The Necessary Journey

What God uses to Push "YOU" into Your Destiny!

---

by

Dr. Kevin L. Harris Sr.

The Necessary Journey
What God uses to Push YOU into Your Destiny

Copyright © by 2015 by Dr. Kevin L. Harris Sr.
Published by Dr. Kevin L. Harris Sr.
1228 NE Magnolia
Lee's Summit, Missouri 64086
Email: getjesussoon@aol.com

Bible quotations are from
King James Version
Scripture quotations marked "KJV" are taken from the Holy Bible, King James Version (Public Domain).

Taken from the **Complete Jewish Bible** by David H. Stern. Copyright © 1998. All rights reserved. Used by permission of Messianic Jewish Publishers, 6120 Day Long Lane, Clarksville, MD 21029. www.messianicjewish.net

Library of Congress Control Number: 2015900126

ISBN-13: 978-0-9864087-0-0

Printed in the Unites States of America

It is easy for people to forget that pastors are congregational members also. Like most pastors, I spent a great amount of time in the pew before occupying the pulpit. That said, I am well acquainted with congregational life. Yes! I have participated in and been a victim of church quarrels. Admittedly there have been times in my Christian walk when I simply wanted to step away. I love Jesus, but at times I fantasized about carrying out God's purpose without the interference of people. Though I spend more time in the pulpit today than I do in the pew, people still confront me with challenges that seem overwhelming.

More than once I have asked the Lord if there is a better way. When Dr. Harris asked me to read his book, The Necessary Journey, I did not anticipate that it would be the Lord's way of answering whether there is a better way. **Dr. Harris, in the most practical and provocative way, has illustrated how Jesus' journey to the cross gives us purpose and direction.** He effectively helps us understand how our journey is tied to Jesus'. Without the path paved for us by Christ we would be lost. This book essentially walks you alongside Jesus as he journeyed to the cross.

Dr. Harris begins the walk in the Garden of Gethsemane. This is fitting because it reminds and instructs us to begin every challenge as Jesus did, in prayer. Whenever tempted to fantasize about a better way, **I will forever be reminded of what Jesus said in Luke 9:23, and this book.** If we are to experience the life God purposed for us, we must do as Dr. Harris has so eloquently transcribed, and embrace The Necessary Journey.

Rev. Antione Lee, *MDiv.*
Senior Pastor,
Central Christian Church
Disciples of Christ

Kansas City, Missouri

TESTIMONIAL

This book is a very simple read. I have read through it (3) times and have found it to be adequately aligned with the life of Jesus the Christ. The progressiveness of each stage actually kept me engaged as to an actual journey that I must experience and have experienced in life.

Seasoned Christians or baby Christians should be able to relate to the examples to allow them to go through various life situations knowing that each stage is necessary in order to make it to their destiny. **This book provides very powerful insight.** The best part about the book, is that I believe it was assigned to me, right now, to read as a part of my journey.

The most powerful insight I received is knowing that I have grown so much spiritually to recognize that some of the things I have experienced was not because I am an outcast or strange, but God was actually working in every situation to prepare me for what was next.

Through this book, God has used a very powerful message to display the necessary experiences that each Christian will face, before reaching their destiny. **This book has encouraged me to gain much strength!**

I fully recommend this book to everyone who has experienced various challenges within the life of church.

Ms. PaQuita Matthews, *BA*
Christian Counselor,
New Vision Christian Church
Disciples of Christ

Kansas City, Missouri

TABLE OF CONTENTS

TABLE OF CONTENTS

TABLE OF CONTENTS

This is an inductive study regarding the life and journey of Jesus, as He approaches His purpose and destiny in life. Each station that He approaches will warrant some type of applicable, response from Him. The journey to the cross is indicative of the Journey of every believer.

Jesus shows us what we are going to face, who we are going to face, where it may likely take place and to whom the opposition may derive. In Jesus last stages, entering into His destiny, His opposition comes from the least likely sources.

At every stage, Jesus shows us as believers how to overcome or deal with each aspect of each stage. As believers we must model the example of Jesus, while we are experiencing each stage and not be surprised or caught off guard as to where the challenge comes from or what must be done in order to proceed through it. As you read through this book you will probably question, why God would allow such pain and agony within the life of Jesus.

Well, it is necessary for each believer to experience these challenges in order to develop our character. God allows it to strengthen us and prepare us for outside, opposition. We are called to evangelize the world and our training ground is within the company of each other. We are to learn from each other and grow as a result of each other.

Odd as it may seem, it works! The Old Testament Priesthood, were instructed to wear their priestly garments, while in the midst of service. Their service was to the believer's, not the outside world. The armor of God should be worn while performing service amongst believers and not to be taken for granted, just because they profess Jesus.

Many make the mistake of letting down their guard in thinking that just because it's a friend, church attendee or leader that they are safe and do not have to be prepared spiritually to protect their heart. You must stay armored up at all times and not be surprised by the offenses that may come from unknown or unexpected sources, especially those of our faith.

With every progression of steps that believer's take it will provoke a certain level of maturity. We will be required to change as well as God changing the situation. If we are not willing to change, then we are not ready to receive the change. God always calls us from the beginning, who; we will become in the end. That means: He definitely sees something within us that He has made us capable of and our confidence in what God says is what reassures us along the way.

When God calls us in the beginning, who; we will become in the end, He does not set us down in the end, but in the beginning. Therefore, we must prepare and be prepared for what God says we are going to become. You cannot skip go and make it to the finish line. There are necessary things that we must go through in order to prepare us for what God ultimately has for us.

Even though we have certain regrets about past decisions, circumstances or situations, God uses it all as a part of our training. That's how: *All things work together for good to those who love the Lord and are the called, according to His purpose.* Romans 8:28

All conflict is not bad conflict. Some things need to be said, done or come to a head. We should not try to prevent something from happening that actually needs to happen.

In each chapter of this book, within each stage, I will ask four major questions.

Question 1: What did Jesus have to go through?

Question 2: Who or What was His opposition?

Question 3: What was the practical example He set?

Question 4: What was the Spiritual significance?

I will reveal the answer to each question, as well as what and how to overcome each obstacle according to the example of Jesus. Again, if you are going to reach your Destiny, you must experience these things.

They are <u>necessary</u> for YOUR Journey into Destiny!

Even though it may not feel good or come from someone whom you have deposited so much into, you cannot be surprised when it comes. God has allowed it! It is designed to grow you up and prepare you for the next step into your destiny.

So buckle up! And let's get ready to take this journey together into The Necessary Journey of a Believer. All of this will be for a specific purpose and in the end you can look forward to Your **RESURRECTON!**

STEP 1

Jesus in The Garden of Gethsemane

Matthew 26:36-41

(Your Prayer Closet)

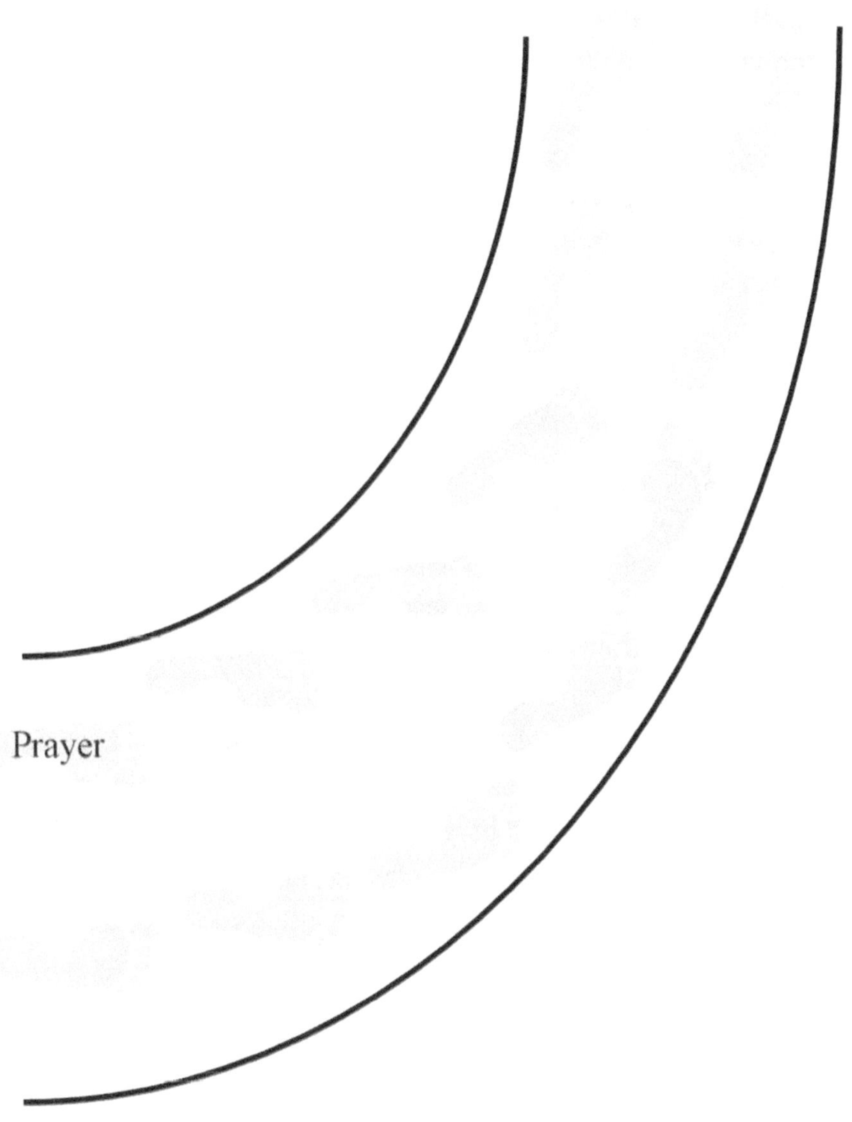

Jesus in The Garden of Gethsemane
(Your Prayer Closet)

Prayer should not be your **last** resort, but you're **First Solution!** The Garden of Gethsemane was Jesus' private, intimate; prayer closet. The Garden of Gethsemane was a place beyond the Kedron Valley, at the foot of Olivet, to the northwest, and approximately a mile from the walls of Jerusalem. Adjacent to it was a garden or orchard. This was a common place of retreat for our Lord, where He would get away from the crowds of people and even His own disciples, in order to talk to God, The Father. This became a genuine place He could take Himself to and get strength for what He had to go thru. Prayer or talking to God is the most fundamental, practice of our faith.

Various things happen, while in the midst of prayer. First, it gives you an opportunity to just express to the Father, how significant He is within your life and how awesome His power and might are within the world or your specific situation. Secondly, it gives you a quiet space where the Father can talk back to you and give you instructions or marching orders concerning your journey. Thirdly, it is a place where regeneration can take place. Where you have poured out of yourself in ministry and you now need rejuvenation or energetic, restoration for what comes next. All of us must not overlook this first step within our journey because we need spiritual, physical, emotional and psychological strength for our interactions within society and mostly ministry.

Notice that the prayer closet is the first and only station where Jesus could take the initiative to willfully take Himself, without being taken somewhere against His will. **No one can really take you to prayer, you must take yourself.** Jesus not only proceeds to prayer, but he invites others to come along and pray for themselves. I will go as far as to say, the reason why many people fail their test is because they did not prepare themselves, through prayer. Look at what Jesus does and says in Luke 22:31-34. *31 "Simon, Simon, behold, Satan demanded to have you,[a] that he might sift you like wheat, 32 but I have prayed for you that your faith may not fail. And when you have turned again, strengthen your brothers." 33 Peter[b] said to him, "Lord, I am ready to go with you both to prison and to death." 34 Jesus[c] said, "I tell you, Peter, the rooster will not crow this day, until you deny three times that you know me."*

Prior to proceeding to His prayer closet, Jesus stops and explains to Simon, Peter that he needs to pray for himself because the enemy will attack him and try to destroy his influence among the other disciples. God always gives warning before destruction and it is His desire to prepare us for our future endeavors regarding our faith. We have to learn to take heed to the warning of the Lord and act upon the instructions given.

Prayer is the vehicle, which collaborates us with God and it is within this premise that God instructs comforts, strengthens and equips us for the unexpected. Prayer with God will reveal some necessary information that will soon become, understood once we find ourselves within the unexpected or expected situation. The light bulb will go off and we will say: Oh! Now I understand why God said, showed or did that.

Prayer is often times laborious. You have to spend some dedicated, intentional time in prayer. As well as: when the Holy Spirit prompts you to pray. A depository, exchange takes place within the confines of prayer. God receives your adoration, explanations, discontents and frustration's. He hears your fervent cry and while you are emptying ou what's bothering you, He begins to FILL you with His Supernatural strength necessary for whatever it is that you are going thru or will go thru.

Prayer can sometimes take thirty minutes to an hour or more just depending on your time frame you have to work with. But once you see the benefits of prayer, it will prompt you to become consistent and laborious in your prayers and it will change the dynamic of your lifestyle and cause you to set some time aside, just for prayer.

Let us look at:
How Jesus prayed?
What He prayed?
And what prayer did for Him?

Jesus prayed with intentionality. He went to Gethsemane for the purpose of prayer and He distinguishes individual prayer from corporate prayer. You must begin going before God on your own, without the accompaniment of others. Your relationship is ultimately between you and God, so you must get use to approaching Him by yourself. Jesus prays on His knees, as an act of submission before the Father. It is His vow of humility before His Father and proves His allegiance to Him. Out of respect to the One who is greater, Jesus bows down before Him.

It is true that we should always be in a mindset and spirit of prayer, but there are times when we need to submit ourselves to prayer, before Him. We are nothing before Him and we should humble ourselves and subject ourselves to the One who is greater! To always stand and pray before God can provoke a spirit of pride within us and cause us to approach Him with some unhealthy, attitude of equality. Get down on your knees and submit yourself to Him and show Him that you give your allegiance to Him. Jesus prays: fervently, to the point that He was sweating profusely. Jesus prays with persistence and consistence! He goes beyond where and how He prayed the first time and then begins to pray the same prayer; again.

In prayer, you must go the extra mile and pray in connection to your desired response. Don't give up in prayer or sell your prayers short. It is ok to pray with confidence, the same thing over again. It does not mean that you don't believe Him, it's because you have tremendous confidence in what you have asked, so repeat with confidence, your expectations before Him.

How did Jesus pray? **Intentionally, with humility, fervently, with persistency and great confidence!**

What did Jesus pray? He humanly prayed: if there was another way for Him to satisfy the sin debt between God and humanity, besides the *Journey To The Cross*. None of us would like to suffer, experience pain, betrayal or rejection. If it was up to us, we wouldn't want to go through anything that would cause so much damage, but Jesus does not end His prayer with the refusal of accepting the pain and agony. He simply says: Not my will, but your will; Oh God, be done! In other words, He gives the Father room to be and do whatever is necessary to accomplish His will before men! What a great vow of allegiance!

Remember, we are limited, but our God is unlimited and how do you think it makes Him feel when we just give Him the freedom to do what will bring glory to His Name?

What prayer did for Him? Jesus' desire to accept what God allowed; brought ministering angels from heaven to strengthen Him. When we do not fight against the Will of God, He will send ministering angels to give us supernatural strength for whatever it is we have to face, thus allowing us to overcome the trial that can be designed to kill us.

Question 1: What did Jesus have to go through?
Jesus had to go through mental agony of what was to happen to Him as a result of His obedience to the Father's Will.

When God gives you foreknowledge or insight, go into prayer so you will not be mentally, antagonized by what can or will happen!

Question 2: Who or What was His opposition?
Jesus' opposition was Himself or His human nature to not respond to what the Father had shown Him.

Overcome your flesh, by not sitting idle when its time to pray!

Question 3: What was the practical example He set?
Immediately, go into your personal, prayer closet and invite those to pray with you who will be affected by what God has shown you.

Question 4: What was the Spiritual significance?
God often uses circumstances to prompt us to building a strong prayer life and we must prepare ourselves to be greatly used by God.
Our trials, often becomes, God's Triumph's!

STEP 2

Jesus Betrayed by Judas and Arrested
Mark 14:43-46

(People Who Reject You and Hold You in Contempt)

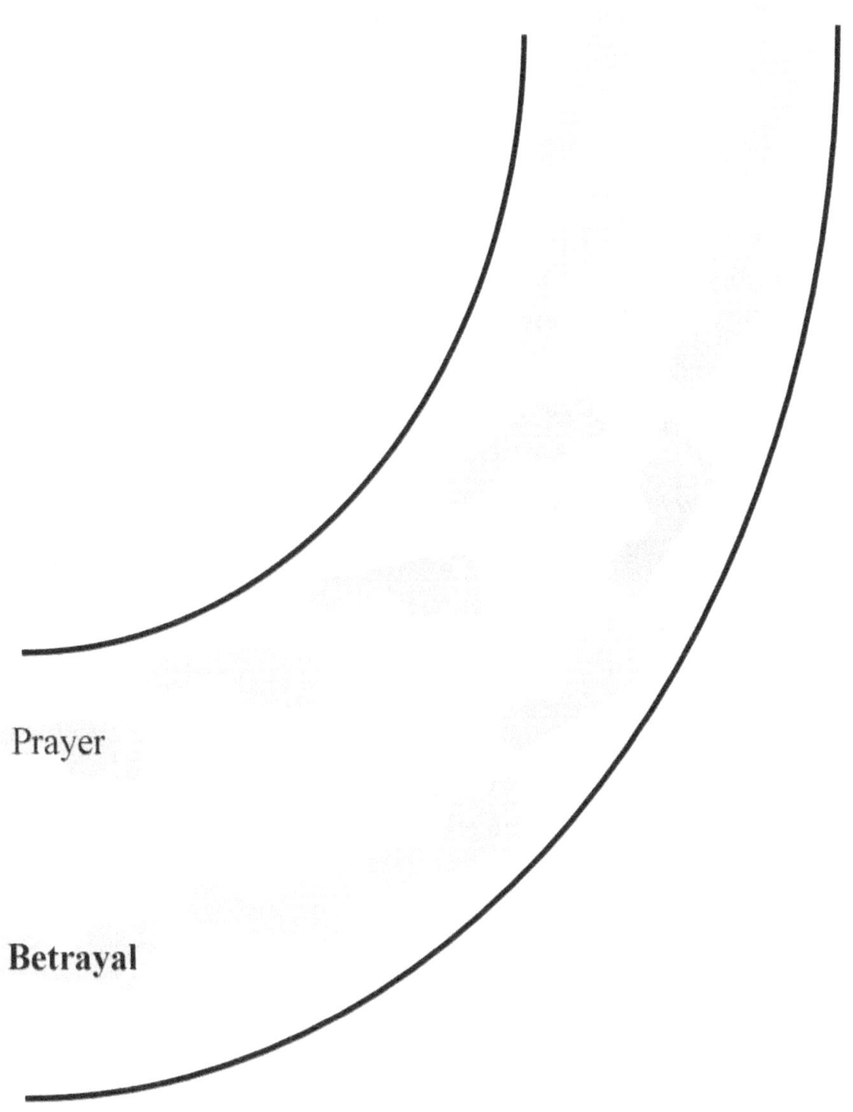

Just when Jesus gets through praying and receiving super-natural strength, His enemy approaches Him in an attempt to betray His friendship. As soon as He finishes praying He hears and sees His enemies coming to arrest Him. It wasn't someone who He did not know or even like. It was the person that He chose as a friend and gave him equal opportunity, just as He did the others, to enter into His inner circle of friendship. Read (**Matthew 26:45-50**)

Jesus strips the enemy of his power by giving him permission to be who he really is. Wow! Jesus said: I see you, know what you are up to and am ready to face your weapon. Can you do that? Can you give your enemies permission to be who they really are? This exposes them before your true friends and empowers them on how to navigate with untrustworthy people. He was betrayed by someone whom He knew and loved. *And Satan entered into Judas who was called Iscariot, belonging to the number of the twelve. And he went away and discussed with the chief priests and officers how he might betray Him to them. They were glad and agreed to give him money. So he consented, and began seeking a good opportunity to betray Him to them apart from the crowd.*
(**Luke 22:3-6**)

Betrayal is only effective, when it is somebody whom you have let into your heart. It doesn't hurt as much if it is someone who you do not know, but when you open up and let your guard down for a close friend and they betray you, it really hurts.

Let's talk about why Judas betrayed Jesus.

It had been prophesied to Jerusalem that a coming Messiah would come and deliver them from their oppression. This coming Messiah would restore their government and rule over their surrounding enemies. However, when Jesus comes as the reigning King, He does not wear a military garment or ride a white horse, but He comes wearing a servants robe and riding on a donkey. His message to His followers was: Bless them which curse you. Love your enemies.

Pray for them which despitefully use you and say all manner of evil against you, falsely. As you can see, Jesus did not look or play the part of which the angry or militant, Jews expected. As a result of this, Judas never accepted Jesus as his King, ruler or leader. That's right! Judas never accepted Jesus from day one and that's why he was never really around on intimate occasions. **The people who betray you, never really accepted you from day one**. They only put up with you and showed up whenever they wanted to.

The scriptures reveal that Judas often stole from the treasury of Jesus and often got upset when monies were not used according to how he wanted them used. This rejection did not surprise Jesus' because He had past evidence of betrayal, leading up to the ultimate act of betrayal.

Stop letting yourself become surprised when the people who never accepted you for who you really are, reject you. Look out for the signs and when you are ready to share intimate conversations and covenant with your close friends, be sure to manage who's in your secret space.

Betrayal is often selfishly, motivated. A person who betrays you didn't just start they have been betraying you behind your back. Betrayal works behind the scenes and then at its most opportune time, it comes out with a vengeance. Betrayal typically does not act alone, but has to be fueled by other entities. Betrayal is deceitful and operates from a cowardly, perspective.

Betrayal is traumatizing and can shatter the mind and emotions of the one betrayed. It happens so suddenly because it has already been planned out. One might ask the question, can betrayal be forgiven? I believe it can, but you must understand that forgiveness is an intentional choice that one makes. Forgiveness should follow a process of: Personal healing, Relationship building, Intentional segments of trusts toward the betrayer and ultimately, forgiveness.

I would imagine it would make it easier for us if we knew who would betray us, but the reality is: we don't know and it's often someone whom we least expect. Jesus knew all things, so He instructed Judas to excuse himself from the table of fellowship and get done what he was going to do. Read (John 13:21-27).

The more Jesus talked about love and forgiveness, the more he became an enemy of Judas. Sometimes, people who do not love or forgive have a hard time doing it themselves and because of their distaste to those acts of generosity, they are fueled by a greater dislike for people. When people are not happy within themselves, they tend to find happiness apart from themselves.

They would rather hurt you, than to even hurt themselves. They get a kick out of seeing someone else hurt, in the same way that they are hurting and find some sense of satisfaction when they have someone else hurting, while keeping them company in a prison of pain. To get through this pain, you must be prayed up or it can very well take you out.

There is no doubt that Jesus was emotionally, wrecked after this act of betrayal, but you must have some spiritual maturity in order to deal with this kind of heartless, act.

People who betray you often have a hard time facing you. They would rather stay away from you than to approach you. It is very difficult for these kinds of relationships to be restored. After Judas betrayed Jesus, he went and threw the money back into the hands of the Pharisees, revealing to us that it never was really about the money, but about a lack of acceptance. Conviction will reveal the true motivation. It will cause you to repent, but your repentance should draw you to the person/s you have affected, not the ones who teamed up with you to commit the crime.

Judas couldn't take it any longer and went and stabbed himself to death. He simply could not face the one he betrayed and would rather no longer exist than to approach Jesus and confess his fault and beg for His forgiveness of him. What I am saying is that, unless you truly want a person in your life who has betrayed you, you typically will not have to worry about them anymore. They will excuse themselves from the relationship and because of the guilt and shame you may not ever have to worry about interacting with them again.

In the event that you do, know who you are and understand that your purpose is too important to allow the enemy to block or prevent it, so you will not become distracted by what the enemy says or does, even if it attacks your character.

Our real enemy, satan knows that he has a short time and if you enter into your destiny, it will pave the way for others, entering into their destiny. If you get distracted and overly, hurt by what someone does, it will hold into bondage everyone attached to your purpose and close the doors of opportunity for them to escape and get on the road to their destiny.

Betrayal hurts, but The Spirit of Lord heals and even though you are hurting right now, your faith can make you whole! Betrayal from your closest helps to push you into your next step of destiny. If you can get past this hurt, you can be strong enough to get past the next hurt. Ultimately, you can really trust no one but God. He will never let you down or damage your character. Character is what causes a person to either trust or not trust in you. Betrayal goes after your character in order to defame your witness or influence within the lives of others.

Ask yourself.

Am I willing to forgive the person who betrayed me and am I ready to face them and confront what happened?

When betrayal occurred, did I back away from ministry or did I continue on, hurting and wounded from the experience? Explain.

Question 1: What did Jesus have to go through?
Jesus had to go through **befriending people, who would never like or accept Him, simply for who He was.** He had to talk with them, eat with them, celebrate with them, laugh with them and sometimes cry with them. He knew who they were, but did not expose them publicly to everyone else. He kept his mouth shut, so that when others would see what Judas has done, it would not be a fault of what He did, but rather a revealing of who Judas really was. In other words, people who betray you will soon show their true colors and you must make sure that you keep your name, clean from any taint of guilt or stain, among your followers or friends.

Question 2: Who or What was His opposition?
Hatred for Him, by the **spirit of satan**, in the **form of Judas** was His opposition. People who hate who you are and what you stand for are the very reasons why people will betray you.

When you stand up for what's right, with the right motive and right attitude, some will despise you for it and intentionally get close to you, so that they can bring you down or impede progress on your influence in empowering others.

Question 3: What was the practical example He set?
Love intentionally and unconditionally! Leave yourself open to accept and embrace anyone who might be willing to change their mind or behavior. When you become aware of their true character, don't put them on blast and attack them first. Don't let your good be evil spoken of. Don't give someone who does not know the full story any reason to find fault in you for doing something out of character, but let them see God in you and become your witness to a loving, respectful and generous person, who only tried to do what was best for any or everyone.

Question 4: What was the Spiritual significance?
 God often allows situations to attack us personally in order **to reveal and develop our true character.** It's easier to get over something when it does not attack your own integrity, but when your name is on the line and what people are saying about you, is not you at all, it can prompt you to say and do some stuff that can bring a stain on you and the Name of your God. Show people that there is something on the inside of you that settles and keeps you! The Holy Ghost will rise up and do what's necessary for the situation!

STEP 3

Jesus is Condemned by The Sanhedrin
Luke 22:66-71

(People Who Judge You, Motivated by Jealousy)

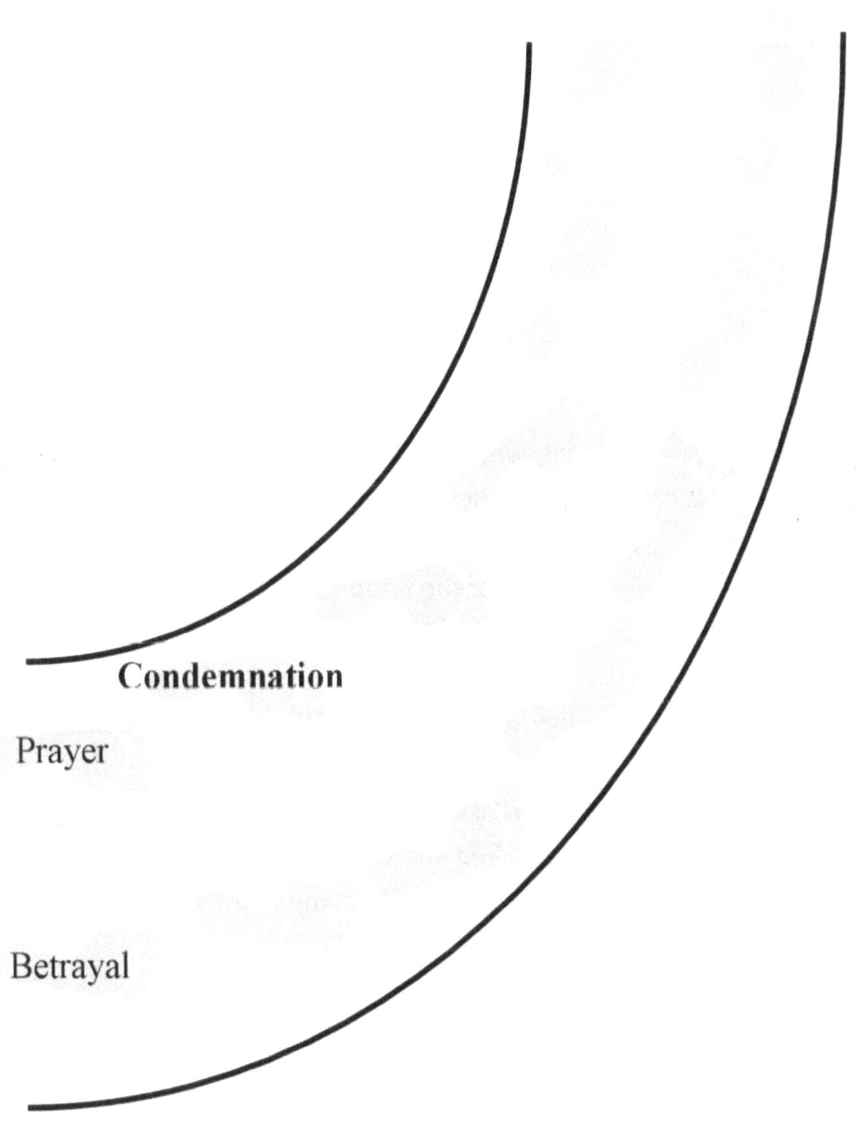

After Jesus is betrayed by Judas and taken captive by the Roman soldiers, He is held in a temporary prison, waiting to be judged by the governing council. It is a struggle trying to figure out why people dislike or despise you for no fault of your own, but because of some unsettled resolve that they have within themselves. Prisons are small spaces that people place you in to contain, prohibit and punish you for how you are exposing their authenticity. They can only hold you there temporarily because it is their plot to hand you off to those of greater authority and persuasion.

This is generally a smaller group or non-authoritative group whose abilities are often inferior to yours. Because they can't stop you, they tattle on you to those that can make a difference and these people are already looking for an opportunity to despise you. Notice that Jesus was held in the prison until daybreak and then taken to the council (Luke 22:66). All of this station's oppression comes as a result of **jealousy**. That's right, when the people that are supposed to support you, can't because they are too jealous of you. The Sanhedrin Council was a group of some seventy-two, Jewish leaders who actually governed the religious rites of the nation. When so called heretics, entered the scene, it was their job to discern and judge their service as either from God or not. If they didn't affirm you, you were not allowed to serve in religious rites as a leader, prophet or teacher.

If you are going to go forward in ministry, they must affirm you and approve that you are from God and can continue on in behalf of the people. Chances are: you will never become approved if they are extremely jealous of you.

Jealousy is when a person becomes envious of another person for whatever reason. Envy builds within a person when he or she consistently sees attributes and abilities within another that seem inferior within the mind and heart of a person. When you can do what they cannot do, they become filled with envy and hatred towards you because of your impact and possible prestige that comes with it. The Sanhedrin was supposed to be the religious, influencers, deliverer's, healers and educators of that time. The church was supposed to be in good shape because of their God-given abilities and authority to lead the church. In this case, Jesus was a heretic and the Sanhedrin had the authority to either affirm Him or condemn Him.

It's one thing when jealousy comes from people who are equally, positioned as you or even lower ranked than you, but it's very different when the people who are jealous of you, are positional, over you. Jesus came healing the sick, raising the dead and speaking with so much wisdom. His impact, authority and power was so much greater than those who were supposed to possess the same qualities, that they became very jealous of Him and tried many times to arrest Him or shut His ministry down. *Before you blame any leader of jealousy, you must be extremely sure that this is it* because the last thing you want to do is harbor a spirit of pride within yourself and think more than what you really are. One way to measure is to observe the genuine, impact you have on others while ministering, while you observe the impact your leader has when he or she is ministering. Genuine impact is not when people are emotionally, louder or active in public service, but when they begin to make real changes in their life, as a result of your gifting.

If you begin to sense and receive rejection from your leader and negative comments towards the way you do certain things or limited use of your gift, chances are: you have entered into a stage of jealousy from your leader/s.

Unfortunately, when its gets to this place it could mean that you have outgrown the ministry in which you are serving and need to relocate by the Holy Spirit's leading, somewhere where you can further develop your gifts. If you stay in a place where the leader/s are jealous of you, it could very well destroy your self-esteem and courage to be used by God. You thank them for what you have learned from them and you move on, with confidence to the next phase of development and ministry for your life.

I know you're asking, why is jealousy, *from the top down* necessary for my journey? God uses this enemy to confront and reveal to the leadership of a church or ministry that they are still undone and have a long way to go in regard to ability and gifting. He also uses it to prove to the leader that they are not always in control, especially when it comes to His Spirit. When a leader loses control and cannot take credit for what is being done, it can lead to jealousy. That's right! It's not so much about you as it is; God is trying to speak to leadership concerning them.

Your ability to surpass this stage is God's constant reminder to the church or ministry that we must continue growing and developing our gifts for the Kingdom. If you stop, as a result of leadership, jealousy, then it's giving them the affirmation that they have arrived.

Churches or ministries are limited in terms of the amount of various gifts that they have within their ministry. And when God sends or rises up someone who can provide what the ministry doesn't have or what it needs in order to grow and service the context in which it resides, He provides a supernatural ability that's either different or more impactful than that of the leader. The leader will either embrace and affirm or become jealous and judge you as a heretic. Let's consider our four questions.

Has the use of your gift truly brought more people to The Lord or matured some believer's within the ministry? If so what have you noticed?

 Is your gift unique to the ministry or is it relatively, common with what already exist within the ministry?

Question 1: What did Jesus have to go through?
 Jesus had to go through being imprisoned and judged, falsely by people who were jealous of Him. God is simply trying to stretch the imagination and ability of another and it just so happens that you are the one He wants to reveal it thru.

Question 2: Who or What was His opposition?
 Church Leadership was His opposition. Trying to gain acceptance and affirmation from those who can control your destiny is a challenge for anyone to face, but you must remember, it is God who holds your destiny in His Hands and if no one else affirms you, He already has!

Question 3: What was the practical example He set?
 The primary, two, question's to Him was: Where did you get your authority? And are you the Son of God?
Jesus remained in silence! When you are operating in the anointing of God, you should never have to justify or defend who you are and what you do. Let your anointing speak for itself! Remain silent and don't say a mumbling word. If they didn't conceive it, they won't believe it and chances are: they will not receive it. But the truth is: they cannot stop it!

Question 4: What was the Spiritual significance?
 Jealousy is a sharp reminder that there is always someone out there who can do it better than you. When someone comes along and can say it or do it better than you, don't shut them out and discredit them. Affirm and validate them because they are a necessary part of your team and because you cannot do it all, by gifting or individually, you will need GOOD help to further you along the way. God says: he that is not against you is for you! Build a strong team of anointed individuals who can minister in various ways to all kinds of people. The greater your gifting, the greater your potential, context.

STEP 4

Jesus Is Denied by Peter
Matthew 26:69-75

(People Who Befriend You, Yet Are Not Spiritually
Mature Enough to Face What You Have To Face)

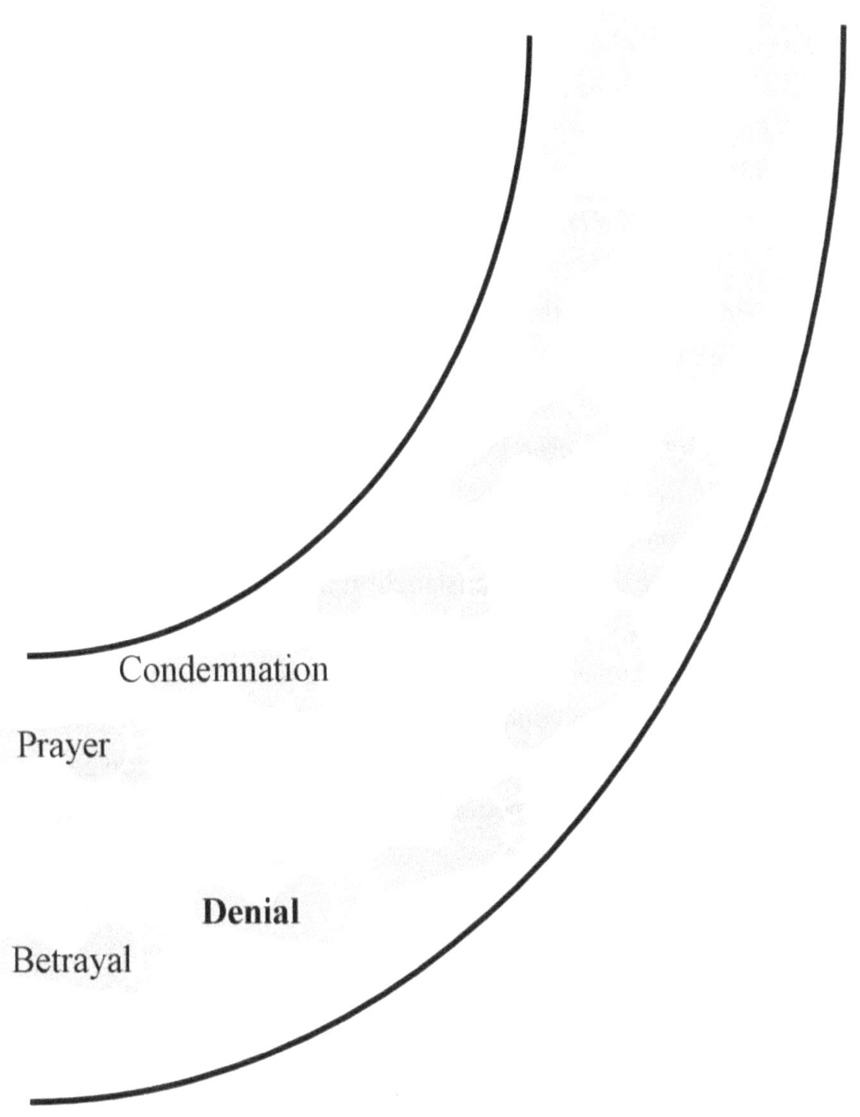

Peter was sitting outside in the courtyard when a servant girl came up to him. "You too were with Jesus from Galilee," she said. But he denied it in front of everyone — "I don't know what you're talking about!" He went out onto the porch, and another girl saw him and said to the people there, "This man was with Jesus of Nazareth." Again he denied it, swearing, "I don't know the man!" After a while, the bystanders approached Peter and said, "You must be one of them—your accent gives you away." This time he began to invoke a curse on himself as he swore, "I do not know the man!" - and immediately a rooster crowed. Peter remembered what Jesus had said, "Before the rooster crows, you will disown me three times"; and he went outside and cried bitterly. **(Matthew 26:69-75)**

First let me say that there is a major difference between betrayal and denial. Betrayal is intentional, but denial is unintentional. People, who betray you, typically hate you, while people who deny you aren't as mature as you. Betrayal is a direct attack against you, while denial is an attack apart from you, directed at the person who denies you. People who deny you just aren't capable of facing the kind of onslaught that you are facing. They are just too spiritually weak or immature in dealing with spiritual warfare or opposition. People who deny you don't mean to hurt you they just aren't ready to walk in your shoes and go where you must go or deal with whatever you have to endure, so when the temptation comes, they deny you because they don't want to face the persecution or the unknown circumstances.

You shouldn't take it personal when someone denies you because they are not rejecting you personally. They are rejecting the confrontation that's in front of them. They are often caught off guard by the enemy and to identify with you means they are spiritually, mentally and psychologically capable of handling the situation. If they plan to walk where you walk, they generally will have to face some of the same obstacles and enemies that you faced. When they deny, it's not you that they are really denying, but it's what you've had to go through that they are denying. When you are betrayed and denied, the rejection often feels, emotionally the same, but in actuality they are two very distinct actions in nature. How do we know? Let's look at Judas's **response to rejecting Jesus** and then let's look at Peter's **response to denying Jesus**.

Judas's Response

When Judas who betrayed him, saw that Jesus had been condemned, he was seized with remorse and returned the thirty silver coins to the head priests and elders, saying, "I have sinned in betraying an innocent man to death." "What is that to us?" They answered. "That's your problem." Hurling the pieces of silver into the sanctuary, he left; then he went off and hanged himself. (Matt. 27:3-5)

Judas's remorse led him to repent to the wrong person. You don't repent to the people you make a bad deal with, but you repent to the person in which you have betrayed. Judas didn't do it for the money, but he did it because he despised Jesus, representing him as his King.

Judas throwing the money back was enough repentance for him, but his conscious would soon get the best of him. People who betray you cannot face you and think that they can just take back what they said or what they did and you should be ok with that. Betrayers will remove themselves from your life because they have a hard time facing the truth.

Peter's Response

Peter remembered what Jesus had said, "Before the rooster crows, you will disown me three times"; and he went outside and cried bitterly. (Matt. 26:75)

Here you find the conviction of The Word of God, reminding Peter of what He said. This moved him to isolation and a time of weeping and lamenting over what he had done. In spirit, he went directly to Jesus and pleaded for his forgiveness and kept himself within the circle of disciples. He didn't leave the fold, but stayed connected to them and kept being reminded of who Jesus is and was, in his life.

Betrayal responds with more rejection, while denial responds with guilt, shame and confession.

Typically, denial will always be preceded by forewarning, that is within the spiritual realm of things. God will often forewarn us of what we need to do before the trial or testing comes. We must learn to take heed to The Holy Spirit when He is leading us to pray, witness, relay a message or etc. We must always be ready!

Instead of Simon, Peter getting prostrate or on bended knees before God, he chose to ignore The Lord's instruction regarding prayer, not realizing that his hour of temptation was just around the corner. Oh! What would the story have been like if Peter would have immediately, begun to pray along with Jesus when He instructed him to? Our stories could be different if we just learn to be obedient and not become lazy in service.

To deny means to disown, to lie, to withhold, to turn back face of or to speak against.

I'm sure that this act of denial hurt our Lord, but Jesus was smart enough to know the difference. Notice that when Judas betrayed Jesus, he did it in His face, accompanied by those who were jealous of Him, but when Peter denied Jesus, he did it behind His back, when Jesus was not around. A betrayal is a setup, intended to blow up right in your face, while a denial often happens behind your back, as a result of supreme pressure from outside sources.

A way to really avoid becoming a person who denies The Lord is to grow in maturity and become a learned, follower of Jesus. We will often find ourselves denying Him when we are spiritually, deficient. When we are prompted to pray, we must pray. When we are prompted to read, we must read. When we are prompted to minister or serve, we must do it. Denial is produced by fear. Fear produces vanity and emptiness. When a person operates out of fear they leave behind their destiny, only to accept mediocrity or they forfeit their dreams and goals.

Remember, when confrontation confronts you, you must be ready to go through the valley of enmity. Someone else is leading the way and the same way they made it, is the same way you'll make it!

Jesus had gone before Peter, within the court of Caiaphas, the High Priest and He was facing judgment. Peter wasn't ready to follow suit, so he disowned and lied knowing Jesus, due to his fear of facing judgment.

Peter denied The Lord three times. The number three represents completeness. Peter completely, denied The Lord in fear of facing opposition. Don't take it personal. Those who deny you can also be easily restored over those who betray you.

After the resurrection of Jesus, He goes to the shore of where Peter and the other disciples are fishing with the intentionality of forgiving and restoring Peter. After a meal, He pulls Peter off to the side and asks him three times if he loved Jesus. Peter, gaining more confidence each time says: Yes! I love you! Jesus ends by telling him to take the lead and guide and instruct His followers. You guessed it. Peter received restoration and a promotion!

Jesus never had a chance to confront Judas because Judas didn't want to face Jesus. When you understand why people do what they do, you can better address the appropriate reaction that's necessary. Those who deny you out of fear can sometimes become your greatest allies! They are motivated by the fact that you did not reject them and have vowed to themselves that they will never do that again. Since you have forgiven them and they have accepted their fault, they will sometimes be your greatest cheerleaders and spend the rest of their time protecting your name, when necessary.

Who do you need to forgive, restore and promote within your own life?

1.

2.

Pray for them and that their faith does not fail!

Question 1: What did Jesus have to go through?
 Jesus had to go through being disowned by someone He tried to prepare for opposition. All of the many efforts and energies you pour into people and prepare them for the enemy, only to find out that they ignore your teachings and warnings and when it's time to make their faith count, they fail the test and disown everything you stood for. This hurts and Jesus did not have time to go back and address it, He just kept moving forward in confrontation, yet emotionally hurting from the denial of His friend.

 Question 2: Who or What was His opposition?
Peter, embodied by the fear of the unknown was His opposition. We must get to a place when it does not matter what we face, as long as we know we have been equipped and that our God is with us!

Question 3: What was the practical example He set?
We must warn and prepare people for ministry and when we see them ignore the signs, know that we will be denied.

Question 4: What was the Spiritual significance?
 Everybody is not ready to face what you have to face, but you must go on through to your own destiny. Your level of spiritual maturity is at a different place than others and you cannot wait on others to get there, but you must pave the way.

STEP 5

Jesus is Judged by Pontius Pilate

Mark 15:1-5

(Unbeliever's, Who Are Appointed By Believer's
to Represent Them)

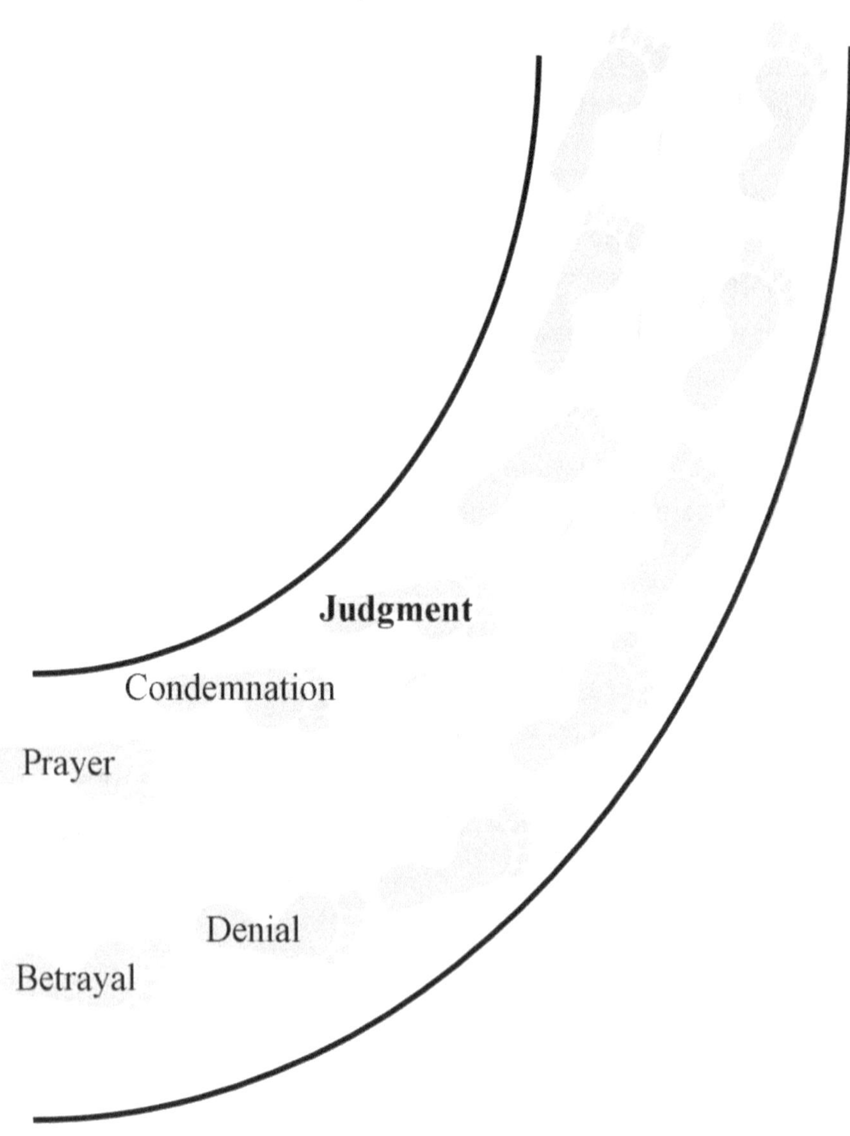

Who is making your case for you or who did you approach to defend your case? Please read: **I Corinthians 6:1-9**

The jealous believer's now hand Jesus off to Pontius Pilate to be judged. A Jew, giving their authority over to a Roman governor or better yet, a believer giving their authority over to a nonbeliever to judge someone who is anointed. Paul writes in Corinthians that this is not the right thing to do. He tries to get his listeners to see the sense in this. Why on earth would you even expect them to have the right motivation, wisdom and godly discernment to make the right decision?

Rome invaded Jerusalem and took it by force and now has set up governance in a land that does not belong to them and now because of jealousy and selfishness of Jews (believers). They hand what little authority they had left and give it to their enemy.

Does this sound familiar? How many believers' have handed their authority of obedience and power of Jesus, over to the devil and allows the devil to state their case? This is absurd, but we do it all the time and expect the devil to have mercy on us. This is where shame and mockery derive from. This is an attempt to shame you or make fun of you in order to reduce your anointing by false witnesses.

In other words, the enemy uses this weapon to take what is real and authentic and make the perception seem false and unrealistic. If people cannot get to you or stop you, they use this method in order to embarrass you, in the hope that you will deny your anointing and forfeit your journey into destiny.

Yes, this hurts your ego, but the only way they can stop you is if you, stop you. Don't ever act like you've never been embarrassed before. If it's not true, it's not you! Don't own the lies that have been told regarding you, by allowing them to stop you. Take a licking and keep on ticking! Who they said you are does not exist, but who you know you are is starring you right in your face. Do you believe the lie or do you believe the Truth?

Here is the undisclosed truth behind this kind of method. The devil, himself knows that he cannot mess with an anointed, child of God and he knows that the only power he has is the power that others give him. He sits back and let believer's go at it in an attempt to bring disgrace to the name of God. There's not much he can do when we are infighting. It just makes the church look bad and that was his motive in the first place. Judgments and accusations are often made by the people, so he loves to throw around he say, she say rumors.

Christian's should not disgrace the name of other Christian's in the company of unbeliever's. This is an antichrist spirit that wedges division between believers' and sows discord into the strand of relationships. This also, gives the unbeliever's a reason not to join in the faith. Notice that when the authority was given to Pilate to judge Jesus, he placed the authority to condemn right back into the hands of the people and they would rather release an unbelieving, murderer than an innocent, humble believer.

Jealous, believer's need the affirmation from ungodly people to justify their need to perpetuate ungodly works. Their works are not accepted by godly people, so they turn to the world for its affirming power to condemn those within the church. They don't bring people to the church to receive Jesus, but they bring them in, already rehearsed with information to discredit the church and or ministry. It's a part of a plot or scheme to discredit the anointing and prohibit the move of God in the ministry. Read (Mark 15:6-15)

Pilate, himself could not find any real evidence as to why the people wanted him destroyed, but the people were filled with jealous, rage and could not stand his anointing. When unbeliever's get to know who you really are, you soon find out that you can have a better relationship with them over the one's you were supposed to have a relationship with. So what am I saying?

God allows this necessary stage of frustration in order to provoke a righteous indignation within us and move us to the ministry of evangelism. Jealousy brought them in, your character built trust, a personal relationship has been established and now they can become converted, as a result of your witness. This is a step in which God uses to build the church! People who would have never inquired upon their own, but have been brought in and end up finding The Lord for themselves. God is always in control!

Persecution often leads us to opportunities of evangelism. We know that to evangelize is to intentionally go out and share the "Good News" with others and share our testimonies about who and what God is, within our lives, but sometimes the opportunity comes by reason of unplanned, divine connections. Pilate was a man of prominence that was brought into a situation that did not initially involve him, but he was able to be introduced to Our Lord and had the opportunity to judge Him for himself. My brother, my sister, you don't know who God is going to bring you into the presence of as a result of your persecution. The fact of the matter is: Pilate needed Jesus, just as much as the Sanhedrin and followers did. Persecution made this opportunity come to pass. Pilate had heard about Jesus and was inquisitive about what he had heard concerning Him. He finally got a chance to meet Him for himself and this was the great opportunity that Pilate had.

Don't get discouraged by what you have to go through, but often look for the great opportunities to witness that come as a result of your false, imprisonment. Pilate did not make the right choice regarding his opportunity, but there has and will be many who will!

Who has God brought you in front of as a result of you being persecuted?

1.

2.

Did you share the "Good News" with them or were you too mad at your accusers?   Yes   or   No   Explain.

Take advantage of every opportunity to share God's Good News!

Question 1: What did Jesus have to go through?
Jesus had to go through **shame and disgrace of someone who is not governed under the same moral and ethical values that He believed.** You can only have fair and just judgment when the person/s you are being measured by are measured by the same standards. Otherwise, what gives someone else the right to judge you, when they are worse off than you?

Question 2: Who or What was His opposition?
False accusations were His opposition. When you are confident in who you are and you are walking in Truth, you understand that outsiders have no power over you and the real challenge is whether or not you are going to bend to what is false or stand up to what is true. Falsehood is designed to lead you out of what is true and force you into becoming something or someone you are not.

Question 3: What was the practical example He set?
 You don't have to always respond to what others are negatively and wrongfully, saying about you. Don't try to defend the Truth, it will speak for itself. **Jesus didn't say a word**, but challenged the outsider to come into his own truth concerning Him.

Question 4: What was the Spiritual significance?
Your works are being judged. Not by you or even the one/s who are judging you, but by the one/s who initially, accused you. Who you are and what you have done is being talked about at a lower level, among equilateral saints and your witness is gaining favor from the bottom up.

STEP 6

Jesus is Scourged at the Pillar and Crowned with Thorns
John 19:1-3

(When You Take The Beaten for The Sins of Others)

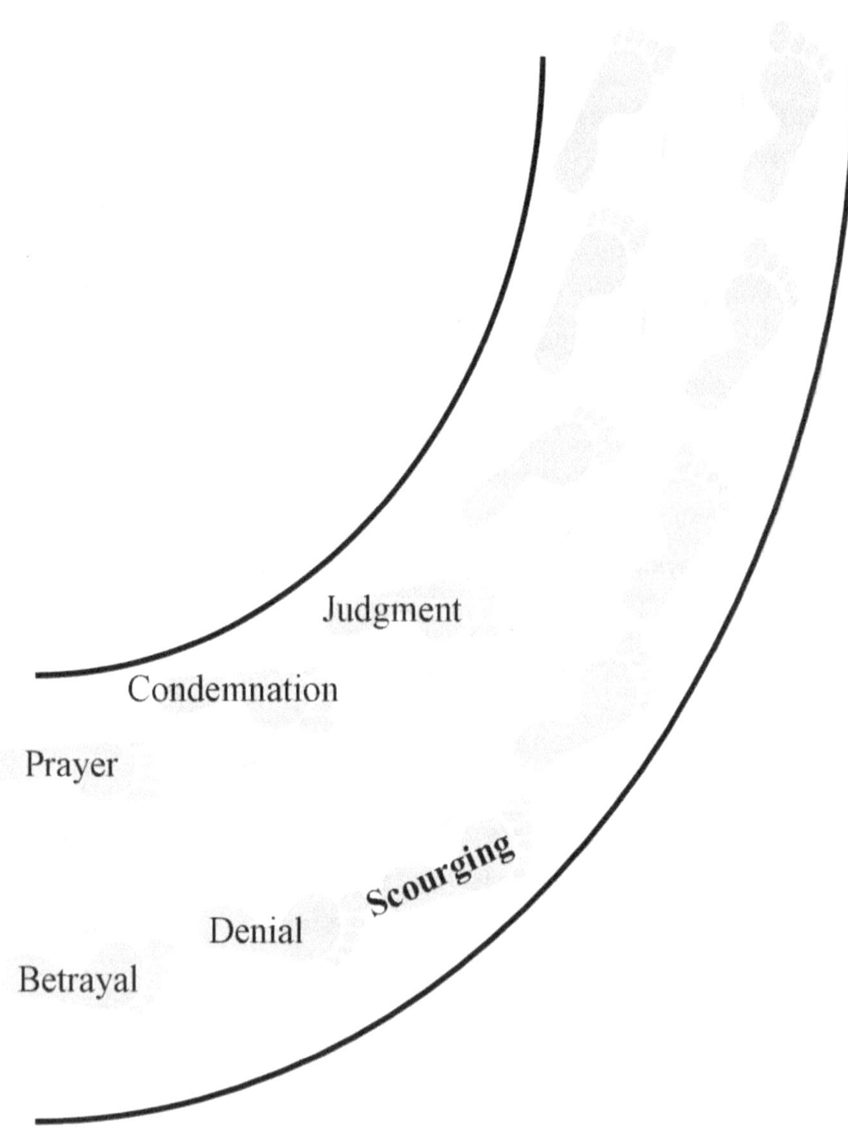

Jesus was physically beaten as well as mentally, emotionally and psychologically, humiliated in front of a crowd. *Pilate then took Jesus and had him flogged. The soldiers twisted thorn-branches into a crown and placed it on his head, put a purple robe on him, and went up to him, saying over and over, "Hail, 'king of the Jews'!" and hitting him in the face.* John 19:1-3 (CJB)

Why would Pilate do such a thing? In his mind, he was doing Jesus a favor by whipping him in public, before His accusers. He thought that if he did this, it would let him off the hook to do anything else, but the initial accusers wanted Jesus dead. Pilate had Him beat as a judgment against His own accusers. Pilate was caught in the middle of a fight between the church and Jesus.

Jesus was being beaten because of their foolishness, but it was necessary because someone had to pay the price for the guilt of the church. Becoming a leader means that you are willing to carry the burden of the church and even when it's not your fault, you will often get the blame. You must have thick skin and broad shoulders when it comes to leadership.

Leadership has its great days, but then it also has its very low days. *"If you can't stand the heat, then get out of the kitchen."* Many want to lead and be seen and receive honor, but very few want to take the responsibility of being blamed, accused, ridiculed or even whipped for the sake of someone else. People will ultimately have to face God for their actions and explain their intents and motives of their heart, but in the meantime, there is another judge and jury that we must adhere to and that is: the world and those who are looking for a Savior.

When the Church is on trial, there must be someone who is big enough, wise enough, mature enough and spiritually strong enough to say: *"If you are going to blame anyone, blame me. I'm the one who is ultimately, responsible for this ministry and therefore, I'll take the fall."*

The outward healing of wounds to the body will generally take the same amount of time, regardless of the person. However, the inner wounds of a beating can take less time to heal, depending on the person. Leaders heal quicker because they have a much stronger, inner man (spirit man) than someone who is immature or a novice. I am not saying that just because a person is a leader, they will always heal faster, but I am saying that a genuine leader, who is spiritually mature can heal sooner because what typically affects others, may not affect them.

Not only was Jesus beaten, but He was also mocked. They placed a purple robe on him and twisted three to four inch thorn branches together and forced it down on his head. This was to embarrass Him as a king. When your accusers and bandwagon opposition mocks you, they consciously do it with your character in mind. If you operate differently than who you say you are, they will typically mock for the opposite but, if who you say you are lines up with your character, they will mock you for who you say you are. Jesus was, is and shall forever be a King and they mocked Him as a king.

Which are you being mocked, the opposite of who you say you are or exactly for who you say you are?

Also notice that Jesus did not try to strip or rid Himself of who they mocked Him to be.

He simply owned or wore their perception of who they thought Him to be. Jesus was comfortable in his own skin and allowed them to prove that He was who He said He was and that even though it was done as a joke, it was still True! Jesus is The King of Kings and Lord of Lords!

As believer's we are kings and priests, therefore, we must act like it, even when we are despised, ridiculed, mocked, abused and beaten. Our character must exemplify that of who we are and no one can take that away from us, even when we are the butt of a joke.

Remember, Jesus is the one who is innocent from the crimes committed between the people, Jewish leadership and so on. All He did was the right things for the right reasons and because of jealousy, envy and hatred; He had to take the fall. Their sin was actually, their sin against God and someone has to pay the price or someone innocent has to atone for someone guilty and that's the only way real forgiveness can take place.

Jesus was beaten profusely, and it seemed like it lasted forever. Forty lashes of sheep knuckle bone, dug into His skin, seven to nine inches deep. Just thinking about it sends chills up my spine and brings tears to my eyes. I am sure it was extremely, painful. Whipping's can be very painful and often detrimental to the mind of the victim. You will have to live with the scars of your experiences and not let them define who you are, but rather serve as testimonies of where you've been and what you've been through.

Don't be ashamed to share your scars. They are introductory doors to began sharing your testimony of what God has brought you through and they are evidence that you have shared in the same kind of scrutiny's that others may find themselves going through. But, you made it!

But, He was wounded for our transgression; He was bruised for our iniquity. The chastisement of our peace was upon Him and by His stripes are we healed! Isaiah 53:5

It was prophesied beforehand, that Jesus would become our sacrificial lamb. I am forewarning you now, that you will have to be beaten and whipped, maybe not physically, but spiritually, emotionally and psychologically for the crimes of others. So get your mind and heart ready because it's necessary for you to proceed to your next level to destiny!

Who has been healed as a result of your sacrificial, beating?

1.

2.

3.

Those person/s have become the witnesses, that you are who you say you are and they have become your tangible, trophies of accomplishment, to present before God as your labor of love!

Question 1: What did Jesus have to go through?
Jesus had to go through literal pain and punishment for being who He said He was and for the crimes of someone else. Don't change who you are or be afraid of what others may do to you. You having to pay the price for someone else's wrongs are persecutions against who and what you know is right. You must stand up for the weak and frail and overcome their evil with good.

Question 2: Who or What was His opposition?
His opposition was **people who are self-centered and empty inside, who love to take advantage of someone else's misfortune and tease them in the process**. Someday they will have to give an account for what they have done to you and it will probably come sooner than later, so let them have their fun now, but payday is coming!

Question 3: What was the practical example He set?
Jesus took it like a man and did not fight against His Kingship. A King is a King, no matter how you slice it. Whether he or she is honored or abused, you cannot change the heart of a King!

Question 4: What was the Spiritual significance?
The enemy will try to steal your royal authority by making you out of a public embarrassment, by identifying you as a sinner or convict. God allows this, so that you can free the slaves of sinners or convicts by your maintaining of a King's mentality. You are not what you've been through, but you are who God says you are!

STEP 7

Jesus Bears His Cross

John 19:15 17

(External & Internal Burdens That Only You Can Carry)

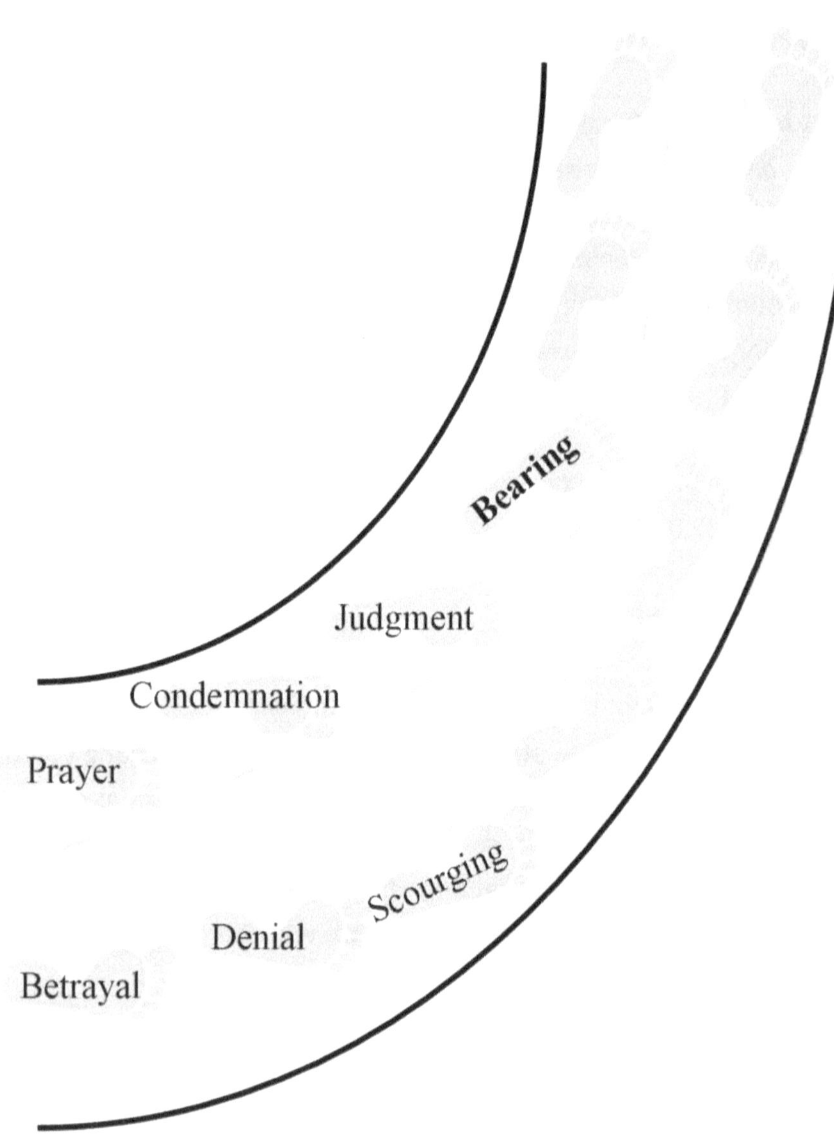

One thing to always remember is that each of us has a God-given assignment. A task that only we, ourselves are responsible for. No one else can fulfill its purpose, but the one who has been chosen to do so. The cross was a cruel punishment that was not a practice of the Hebrew people, but a Roman practice of execution. The cross symbolization was partly that of: rejection. No matter who you were, when found guilty of committing a crime, you were rejected by the people.

When you have to carry your cross, it is partly symbolic of carrying rejection. All that has happened to you in regard to persecution is indicative of the rejection that you have had to endure.   Your cross is a mixture of joy and pain, happiness and sorrow, life and death. Your cross has your name on it and it is your responsibility to prepare yourself to carry this physical, spiritual, emotional and psychological burden that is assigned to your personhood.

Notice that the actual cross was a physical (external) weight that was visible to everyone around to see. The things that people actually see you doing are visible images of your responsibility that people love to place upon you. It's not so much, your weight, but weight's of other people, forced upon you. That's really all that most people see and they write your work off, as if you are supposed to do it or it's not too much for you to bear.

However, what they cannot see is the mental (internal) weight that is weighing you down on the inside. The external stuff is much easier to carry than the invisible stuff that's overloading your ability to cope.

The external and internal weight, together make it almost impossible for you to carry. When you are weighed down from the inside out, it can cause you to lose your mind and forfeit your journey. This is where the "why me", statement comes from and this is why many people never make it to their destiny because of the overload that is upon them.

Scripture says: *No temptation has seized you beyond what people normally experience, and God can be trusted not to allow you to be tempted beyond what you can bear. On the contrary, along with the temptation He will also provide the way out, so that you will be able to endure it.   I Cor. 10:13* (CJB)

The physical strain is not nearly as heavy as the mental strain. The mental strain is what produces strokes, heart disease and etc. All of the experiences that you have had in life, prior to this spiritual cross is what has shaped and prepared you for what you are facing now and you must not forget how you overcame the previous struggles that you have been thru.

It is extremely important to know the strains that have been assigned by God, verses the strains that you have put on yourself. The good thing to know is that God can use them All to His Glory for your life! Yes! In spite of: He can turn your troubles into triumphs! Strain's that you put upon yourself are usually identified by their relation or correlation to the spiritual things.

Remember, the weight that Jesus was carrying, physically was figurative to the weight He was carrying inwardly (the sins of the world).

When you can match what you are going through, naturally with what you are going through, spiritually that's one way of deciphering, whether or not it's assigned by God or placed upon by oneself.   If there is no spiritual resemblance than chances are, you are overloading yourself. When you can make the connection, there is always a bigger picture and it is God's job, through the Holy Spirit to reveal to you the purpose and the outcome.

You have to make sure to focus on carrying your own cross, rather than someone else's cross. The one thing we can never regain back is time. Time will always proceed and we must not be caught in regression or stagnancy. You cannot waste time carrying a burden that's not yours because you will soon find out that when God assigns a cross to bear, it's wasted effort trying to help someone beyond God's boundaries of assistance. When God says: no, there is nothing anyone can do to make it a yes or vice versa.

God is either causing something to happen or He is allowing something to happen and when we get in His way, we only prolong the process within the journey. Burdens are heavy, often times much greater than our capacity to handle. That's why we need a supernatural force to rise up within us and help us to carry that which is too much for us to carry. It's not so much about your physical (outer) strength, but more about your spiritual (inner) strength.

People on the outside can't really understand how you can carry the weight's you are carrying because they cannot see or even control your inner strength. This is always an opportunity for you to share your faith, when people see you coping beyond human ability and accrediting you with a power that seems to be operating within you.

One of the misperceptions regarding carrying your cross is that you must continuously smile and ignore what and how you are feeling. Do you think Jesus smiled all the while He was carrying His cross or do you think He expressed grimaces of pain, agony, frustration and heartache. You can be real and honest about how you are feeling, while carrying your burden, without thinking you are letting The Lord down.

He wants the truth. Even though it hurts and causes you pain, you can still make it! You will not be judged on how you looked, while you went through what you faced, but you will be judged on whether or not, you overcame what you faced. It's not about being happy all the time, but it's about enduring, even though you are unhappy. It's about defeating your feelings of giving up and throwing in the towel.

You were made to be a winner and as long as you have The Lord on your side, you are victorious! Sometimes our failures are God's successes. What I mean is that, when you naturally fail, God will allow you to spiritually succeed! When He is teaching us about His Divine Providence, He often shows us, despite who we are or what we are going thru, our own efforts can cause much exhaustion. He proves to us that He is able and often the only one who can fix our situation.

Always look for the good out of bad situations and be sensitive to the spiritual significance or revelation that the Holy Spirit is trying to get you to see. Life lessons are not by accident, but learning opportunities by which we can grow!

Question 1: What did Jesus have to go through?
He went through a time of public display of carrying his burdens, both inwardly and outwardly.   Most people will only understand the physical burden because that's what they see, but they won't understand the spiritual because it's happening beyond the naked eye. Many people are looking at you and making their assumptions, but you must carry on with much dignity!

Question 2: Who or What was His opposition?
Public shame and embarrassment was His opposition, embodied by the soldiers who whipped Him along the way. It's one thing to be judged and condemned, but it's another thing to be tormented along the way. They will torment, persecute and criticize you along the way, but the Truth is in your Outcome! The Truth always prevails!

Question 3: What was the practical example He set?
Don't focus upon the external, but the internal. Your mind must be renewed because it is the place where God will give you strength to carry the external. You are stronger from the inside, not the outside. When necessary, people have been known to carry or pick up things one hundred times their weight because of an inner strength.

Question 4: What was the Spiritual significance?
The natural man cannot obtain spiritual things. When you are naturally focused, you cannot identify the spiritual force behind what's happening in the physical and as long as the spiritual enemy goes unidentified, it can continue to reside in the caves of your hidden heart. Expose him!

STEP 8

Jesus Is Helped by Simon of Cyrene
Mark 15:21

(People Who Are Assigned to Assist You
in Carrying Your Burden)

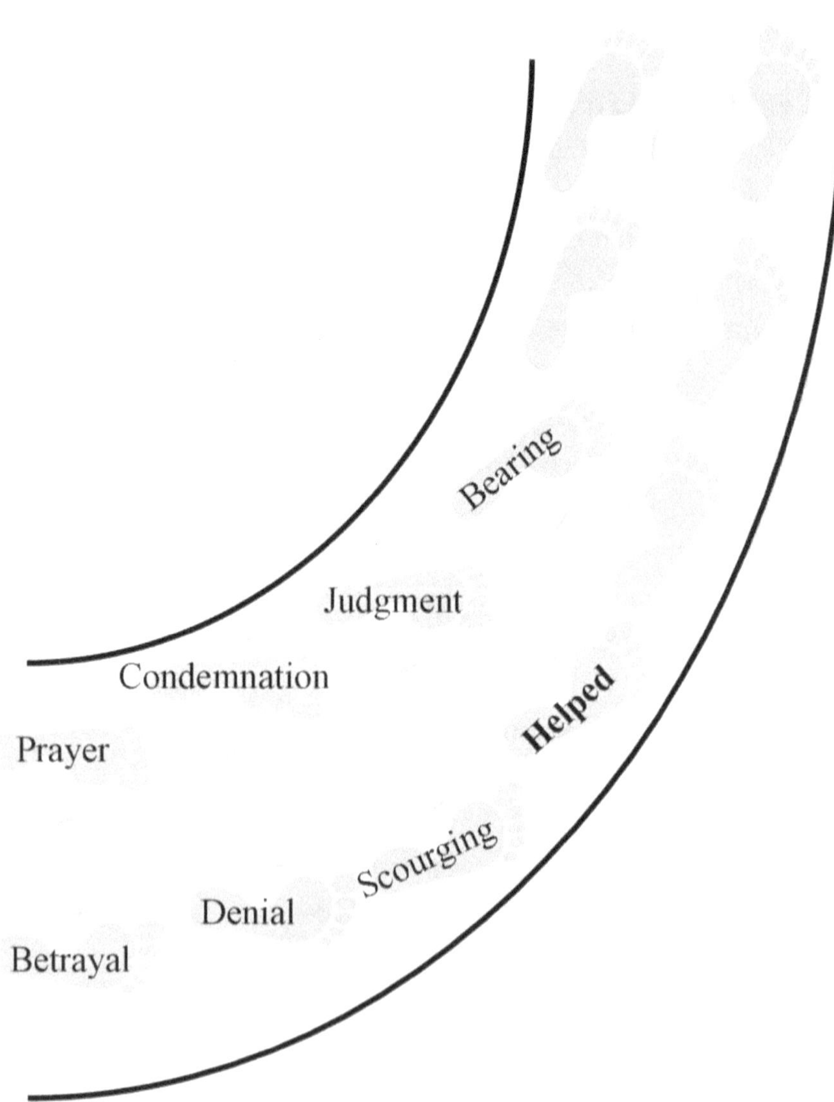

A certain man from Cyrene, Shimon, the father of Alexander and Rufus, was passing by on his way in from the country; and they forced him to carry the stake. **Mark 15:21** *(CJB).* When it looked like from the natural perspective, that Jesus was having some difficulty carrying His cross, the enemy chose a man out of the crowd, not of the same ethnicity, culture or nation and enforced upon him to carry and assist The Lord in bearing His burden. This is a very interesting and intriguing principal within the entire process of the journey.

Just as well as you have goals, the enemy has a goal as well and he is only satisfied at your complete demise. Therefore, he is willing to help you make it completely to your demise and will even try to speed up the process by offering temporary, assistance. That is the spiritual, overtone that's working behind the scene of this stage within your journey. While your enemy is at work, so is your God! God is also meeting the need of the stranger, by allowing him to be in the right place at the right time to come into acquaintance with his Savior.

Simon was inquiring of Jesus and went up to the Feast of Passover to see Him. Never in a million years did he figure, he would get up close and personal with Jesus. Simon represents the many people who are not satisfied with life as they know it and are looking for a deliverer to save them from their own selves and give them a new sense of identity and existence. When a curious person gets close enough, they could very well be called into the game.

Because the enemy is only looking at the natural, he demands assistance from a natural perspective. God connects the Savior with the one who is lost and gives the lost validation of who they are and what they bring into this new relationship.

In this stage of natural assistance, God often sends you help from someone you would least expect or that you may not even know in order to show you that He understands where you are and that you need help in carrying your load of responsibility. This can be attributed to a minor break within your journey and an opportunity for you to get refocused, replenished and renewed, so that you can finish your course.

So now that you have been given a break, what are you going to do with it? You must make the best use of your time, not by complaining or looking for a way out, but by praying, fasting, acknowledging God's presence, seeking wisdom and direction and ultimately, gaining new strength to finish what you started. This break is a short break.

This break allows the stranger to experience a little of what you go through and feel the level of sacrifice that you are making on their behalf. This is how we come to know Jesus as our Savior, by receiving His love and sacrifice for us. Not collectively, but personally. This new help becomes more inspiration for you as you retake your cross and finish your course. God shows us that our labor is not in vain and every step we take, there are new people that will become involved, whom you have impacted and they will lighten the load and assist you in this great endeavor that's before you.

A person who is genuine and have given themselves as a sacrifice will never forget those who helped them along the way and they will be forever in the heart and mind of those who needed help, when they needed it the most. Simon could now feel the responsibility of doing his part and become an equal share in this journey. When people can experience your heart, they often adopt your journey for their journey and they can become lifelong partners in the adventure of your journey.

This was certainly not the intent of the enemy, but because he is a deceiver and a deceiver of himself, he could not for see what would become of this joint venture. What the devil meant for bad, God turned it around for good! The devil is so concerned about you failing that he won't discern the friends you will gain along the way. God is always in control and you must see Him at work, during your time of heaviness, strain and indignation.

When you feel, receive or sense a minor break or when God sends you some assistance, maybe even assigned by the enemy, do not be mistaken to think that your time or season is over, but that this is a temporary water break and you must be ready to get back in. This is not an extra burden or new burden, it's the same one you had from the beginning, and you just have to finish the course. Many people think that God is punishing them or that more bad things keep happening and they don't quite understand that this is the same game, just a different quarter. It's almost over, but you have to keep going until the last whistle blows.

This is what I call the "Deception cycle". The enemy wants you to think that you are in a new trial or new burden, when in actuality it's the same one you've been in all along. He wants to defeat you in this cycle and make you think you will never get out and that this must be all it is for you. But don't be deceived.

All of what you are experiencing is a part of the necessary journey that you already began. If you have to keep starting over than you would think you will never make it to the finish line and that's what the enemy wants you to think. You are closer to your break through than you've ever been, so get refreshed and get back in the game and finish your course!

When God sends assistance, assigned by the enemy, it is important that you completely take hands off, so that the stranger can completely put hands on. The stranger will never fully appreciate the journey if you continue to keep your hands on it. They need to feel the pressure of what it's all about. When you keep your hands on, it diminishes the amount of wherewithal that it takes to function and gives them a un-appreciation or misunderstanding of what it entails to carry such a great responsibility. This is a time for God to reveal Himself to them, in a way that provokes their faith and causes them to build trust in their God.

You rob them and yourself of this opportunity for God to really be God in their lives. Here is a question you must consider.

To who have I overly compensated and sheltered from the realities of experiencing God for themselves?

1.

2.

I must let go and let God!

Question 1: What did Jesus have to go through?
Jesus had to go through watching someone else carry a heavy burden that belonged to Him. This is a time to analyze and observe and this will help you to appreciate, "you" for all that you do. You are not God and therefore, you cannot decide for them how strong they are, they have to find that out for themselves.

Question 2: Who or What was His opposition?
Jesus opposition was his own need to jump in and remove what was presumably, too heavy for Simon to carry. I know you want to help. I know you want to lighten the load. I know you want to fix it, but how would God prove to them how strong they are and how strong God is?   I know what seems so heavy for you, my seem too heavy for someone else, but let them struggle with it for a while.

Question 3: What was the practical example He set?
Don't push people out of the way who have been assigned to help you. Scoot over and let them help. Jesus focused on the cross and knew that it was not over for Him yet, but He went further in His mind to the end result.

Question 4: What was the Spiritual significance?
God will save someone's life in the midst of your own struggles. He will use a conflict to create a case study chronicle for the "Church" and show us how to build the local church, through relevant ministry! When you become their savior, it removes the glory from God and God will not share His Glory with anyone!

STEP 9

Jesus Meets the Women of Jerusalem
Luke 23:27-31

(People Who Are Supporting You
As You Go Through Tough Times)

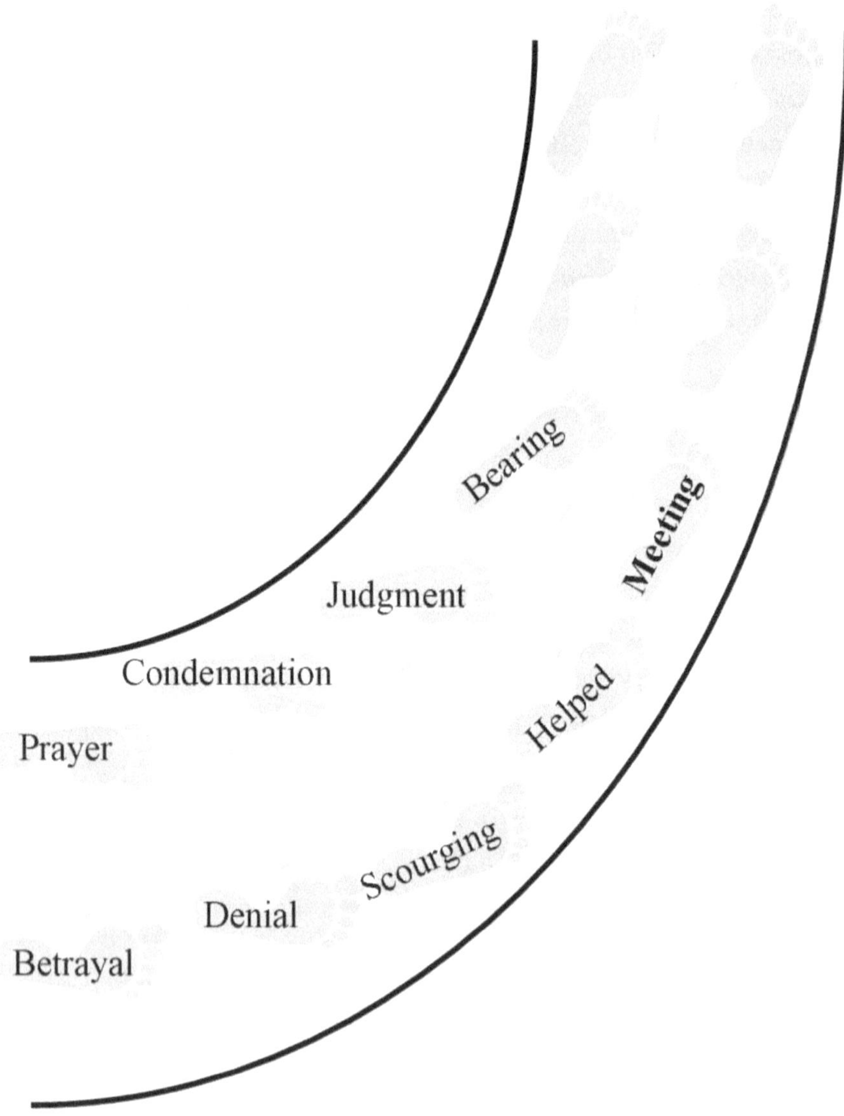

The journey that you are on, usually feel and seem like a very lonely journey. Even though there may be people around you, it often feels like nobody could possibly be going through what you are going thru. This is an emotional attempt, by the enemy to make you feel isolated within the confines of your own mind and cause you to develop an insecurity complex.

One very important thing you must remember is that there are people who are supporting you, while you are going through whatever you are going through. ***Everybody is not against you***. And you must be able to pinpoint your support system in the midst of a hostile crowd. There was a small pocket of people within the midst of a large group of people, who truly supported Jesus as he suffered.

During this time within the western culture, women were considered second class citizens and did not have equal rights of walking alongside the men and the priesthood. Women have a tendency to feel a certain amount of compassion and emotion towards others when they are going through. However, there are people who genuinely, care about you and support you, completely in the midst of your storm.

Remember, this is the time when Jesus has been given a temporary break and a brief moment to catch His breath and regain new strength. Just because you get a break doesn't mean that you are off duty. This is the time for you to now encourage your support system and let them know that you are ok and that they can make it as well. Jesus turns to them and tells them not to weep for Him. What an amazing request by a suffering Savior!

What an opportunity to show the ones who are looking up to you a sign of spiritual strength and fortitude. During this stage it is important that you testify to those around you and give them a sense of hope within a hopeless situation. He also begins to prophetically speak to them concerning their future. After you go through the experience of carrying your burden and God gives you a temporary break, you now have the experience to share with others who will suffer as well and God will give you insight into the expectancies of others and give you words of encouragement out of your mouth.

He shares with them that many people will try to avoid or wish this day would never come for them, but Jesus encourages them that they can make it and to look to Him for courage and strength. You cannot bottle up and not release encouragement during this stage of your journey. This serves as an outlet for you to release the anxieties that are within yourself and inspire yourself, by inspiring others. You must not keep your mouth closed during this time because you may not get an opportunity to speak as you take back up your cross and finish the race.

Timing is everything! When the load was lighter, Jesus took that time to witness and share with others who were supporting Him. All they could do was lament and mourn with Him. I'm sure they were saying amongst themselves and within themselves, why Him? Why? Does He have to go through all of this pain and suffering? He didn't do anything to deserve this and I wish it was me, instead of Him.

Jesus had to settle their nerves and calm their fears and help them to understand that there was absolutely, nothing they could have done to prohibit this from happening, but it was necessary for Him to go through this and experience this, on behalf of them. They wouldn't quite understand it now, but they would later on. People will not quite understand, "*why*" you are going through this, but as God reveals the bigger picture, they will remember your words and testimony and prophetic utterance, when you were going through your trial.

This can be a very, very emotional time for you and your support system. You must remember that they will not want to see you in the state that you will be in during this stage and it is very important that you do not let them talk you out of finishing your course. Their tears and moans will provoke great, sensitivity within you and it can become only natural to just ease their pain, by walking away. Your sacrifice is necessary for their deliverance. You are doing this for them and for those who will come after them, so you cannot abort your burdens just because of how its making them feel.

Stay the course and finish your purpose. If it was up to them, they would eliminate all of your enemies, snatch you away and take you home and nurse all of your wounds. Particularly, if it's someone really close to you, like a parent, sibling, spouse, family member, neighbor or etc. You must remain committed to your cause and prepare them for whatever they will have to face because it is necessary that you go through this trial.

As I am writing this book and thinking about this stage within my own life, I'm thinking about the many times people have told me that what I am going through is not necessary and that I can just quit and go somewhere else or do something else. They were only looking out for my best interest, but they did not consider that this was all permitted by the hand of God and that it was completely, necessary that I experience this stage within my ministry. As they jockey and try to build allies for you and discover who is really on your side, you must remind them not to divide people, but rather show forth genuine loving-kindness to everyone.

Your heart is available to all, even your enemies, as their heart is only open to those who express total commitment to you and them. You must remind them to love their enemies and pray for those who despitefully use them and say all manner of evil, falsely against them or you. Teach them how to express unconditional love, when your own love is misunderstood or rejected.

Time is just about up. You have gotten a little break and some well needed assistance. You have encouraged those who love and support you and now it's time to relieve your temporary help and take back up your cross and finish your assignment. Be sure to thank and affirm the one/s that helped you and let them know their labor was not in vain.

When I was going through this stage of my journey, did I come across to my support system as encouraging or humiliated and defeated? Circle one.

Yes   or   No

How did I respond?

What could I have said or done differently, now that I have a better understanding of this stage of ministry?

 Question 1: What did Jesus have to go through?
Encouraging others who did not quite understand "why" or for what reason was He going thru? They love you as the man or woman and at this juncture, they don't really care about anything else. You must show them the spiritual side of which you are and help them to accept what God allows.

 Question 2: Who or What was his opposition?
His opposition was the power of silence. Would he speak of persuasive, positivity or would he hold his peace and have nothing of assurance to provide?

Question 3: What was the practical example He set?
He immediately, turned to those who loved and supported Him, while He had the time because the opportunity to do so could very well pass Him by. Look past their pain and prophecy to their spirit and prepare them for what lies ahead.

Question 4: What was the Spiritual significance?
Satan knew that if he could silence Jesus during this time, he would discourage those who were following and pierce their faith. The Truth always has the last say!

STEP 10

Jesus is Crucified

John 19:16-24

(To Be Bound, Affixed, Then Suspended In The Public Eye)

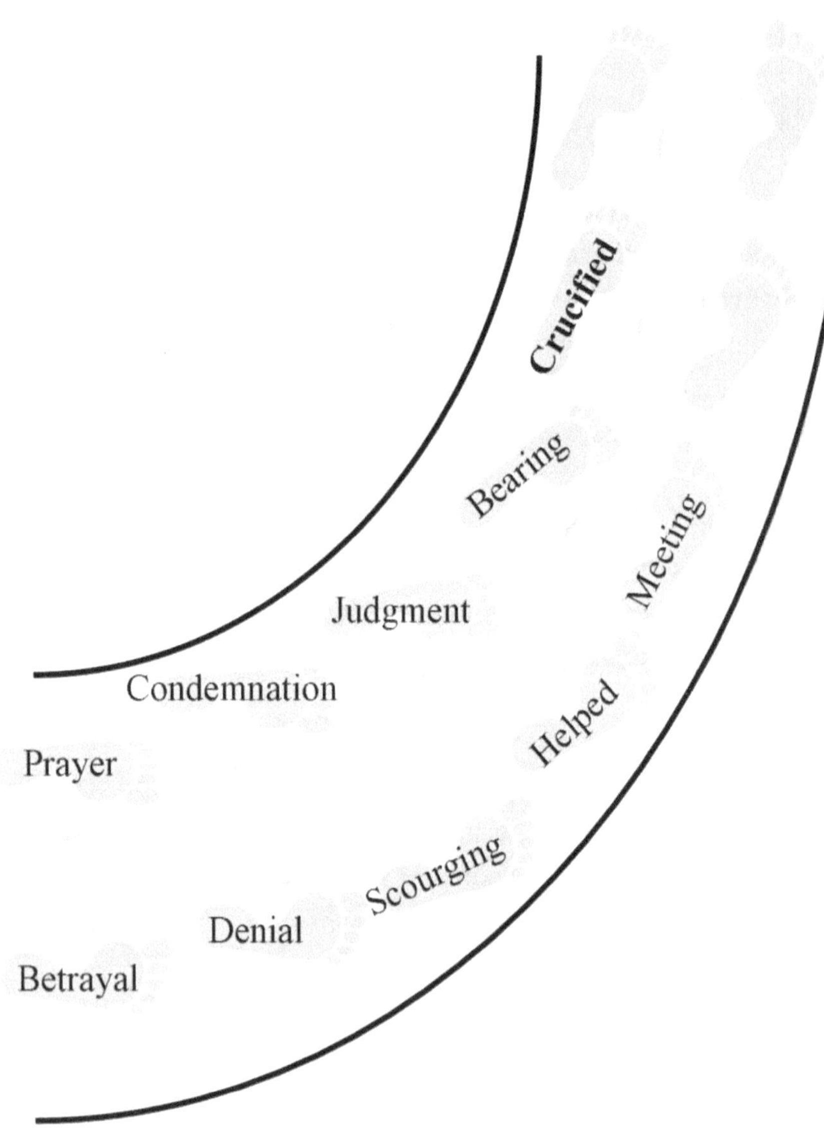

This form of punishment was extremely cruel and used in extreme cases, where the convict deserved to die a harsh, excruciating, slow, but very painful death. This kind of punishment was reserved for the worst kind of citizen meant to be a public disgrace. Your hands were affixed and your feet were affixed, thus causing you not to be able to move or catch your normal breath. You could hang out there for days, before you actually died and it involved tremendous, torture.

First of all, Jesus did not deserve to die this kind of death. His alleged, violation was not deserving of this method of punishment. It's one thing to be found guilty of a crime that you did not commit and have to suffer from this kind of scrutiny, agony and pain. It is during this stage that you say to yourself, *did it really require all of this?* This is the stage where you suffer humiliating, public, pain. The enemy wants to make you a public example and set a standard for how it will torture you if you go against the system of its operation.

This is when it really hurts. It's easy for us to hurt when we are in the privacy of our own environments, but it's another when we are made a public, spectacle and ridiculed in the eye of the public. People who never even had any thoughts about us have now been forced to make them because of the situation they have now seen us in. This is when, it's really not fair.

What did you do to deserve this? All you tried to do was the right thing, but those who were threatened by your abilities and anointing have now criticized you severely and unrelentingly. No matter what you say or do, there is no way out. You can't pray your way, talk your way or wiggle your way out. You are stuck and nailed to the wall of persecution and if that's not enough, people are walking by and making fun of you and what you are going through. They don't have all of the information and have made the assumption that if you're going through this, it must be something wrong that you've done.

You didn't think they would take it this far, but they did and there is absolutely, nothing you can do about it. When you are operating under the anointing and bringing deliverance to those who have been enslaved, broken and under captivity, the enemy puts a hit out on you and the only way he will be satisfied is if you were put to death. He wants to make sure, you will never have any kind of positive impact again, and he takes you through the worst of the worst, kind of torture and pain.

Can you take it? Even though it wasn't your fault, can you sit there and take the pain of criticism, agony and heartache? *Jesus did!* There would be no acquittal or reversal of the conviction. Remember, a price has to be paid and you have been the one assigned to cover the debt. God has made you for this and anointed you to go through this. God is with you and the pain you are feeling now will not be compared to the joy you will feel later, whether in this life or the life to come.

Lest you think the enemy is getting off scot free, he is constantly being tormented by the Truth. When they wrote a notice and posted it on His cross, it read, *Jesus from Nazareth, The King of the Jews!* Jesus was crucified for who He said He was all along and Pilate (His enemy) could only pen what was true. Are you willing to die for who you say you are? If so, people will recognize you for your unwavering faith and belief in who you say you are.

Whether good or bad, you will always be known for who you are. Many people were convicted by the saying and wanted it taken down, but Pilate was spiritually, prohibited of taking it down. *It is, what it is,* he replied*!* I'm sure Jesus screamed and yelled when He was being affixed to the cross, but He did not yell back, call his enemy a bad name, curse or swear or tell His enemy to let Him down and let Him go.

Jesus' grunt and grimaced, but took it like a soldier. What you are going through as a vessel of God is necessary for your journey be-cause if you never know what it's like to experience public, scrutiny, humiliation or pain, it would be quite difficult for you to reach those who are afraid to do the right thing that goes against the worlds way of doing things. Jesus is an example to us that when we do it God's way, everybody is not going to like it and what use to be normal, has now become abnormal and wrong is now right, and right has become wrong.

Jesus stood for what was right and never compromised His belief. Even if it meant, public humiliation. I know the darts that people are throwing at you, hurt. I know the words that they are hurling at you are wounding your self-esteem. I know the false accusation's they are placing upon you don't even fit your character, but you are over-coming the power of their plan, by not lashing back, giving in or giving up.

When Jesus was suspended in the air or in public view, the enemy's army tore up his garments and stole His priestly robe. They had no appreciation for his outer clothes, but have sacred appreciation for his priestly, robe.

Isn't that simply amazing? The priestly, robe was said to be seamless. In other words, it was consistent from the top to the bottom. There were no stopping points at all and this is the kind of service that God requires of us; godly, consistency. When your character has this kind of quality, even your enemy will respect and reverence it!

The scripture says: they gambled for which one would take the robe. Now, whoever won it and didn't value it now, would probably value it later, once they've come to know who Jesus is and was. Your consistency may not look like its paying any dividends now, but it will surely pay off later. Make the enemy respect your anointing, even though he may not respect you as a person, he will not be able to deny your sacred place.

Here is Jesus, hanging in suspense and looking down, over the crowd of naysayers, supporters and enemies. He is looking hopeful, while hurting. Are you a sign of strength at your most vulnerable and weakest moment?

When you have gone through this stage, what have people said concerning your character?

Is your faith and character, consistent or are there some pin holes and shriveled strings within your character?

What are they?

Question 1: What did Jesus have to go through?
**Jesus went through the public perception of being totally rejected
by society.** When the majority rules and it's not based upon each
individual, but by those in authority, will you still hold your head up
in the midst of humiliation?

Question 2: Who or What was His opposition?
Self perception was at stake. Regardless of what everyone else is
saying about you, what are you saying about yourself? What
matters most, is what God thinks of you and what you think of
yourself.

Question 3: What was the practical example He set?
**Hold your head up and don't be afraid to look your enemy in his
eye or your support system in the eye or the naysayers in the eye.**
The price you are paying is not because of what you did, but because
of what your enemy did and because you are the sacrifice, you must
love, unconditionally.

Question 4: What was the Spiritual significance?
**God hates sin. Therefore, when Jesus was hanging in suspense, He
was rejected by the world, as well as sin, rejected by God. It was a
feeling of not being wanted by anybody.** God hates the sin, but
loves the sinner. Jesus hung in our place and God received His
sacrifice for us. **God accepts, what the world rejects!**

STEP 11

Jesus Promises His Kingdom To The Good Thief

Luke 23:39-43

(Prisoners, Who Will Affirm and Defend You During Your Worst Moment)

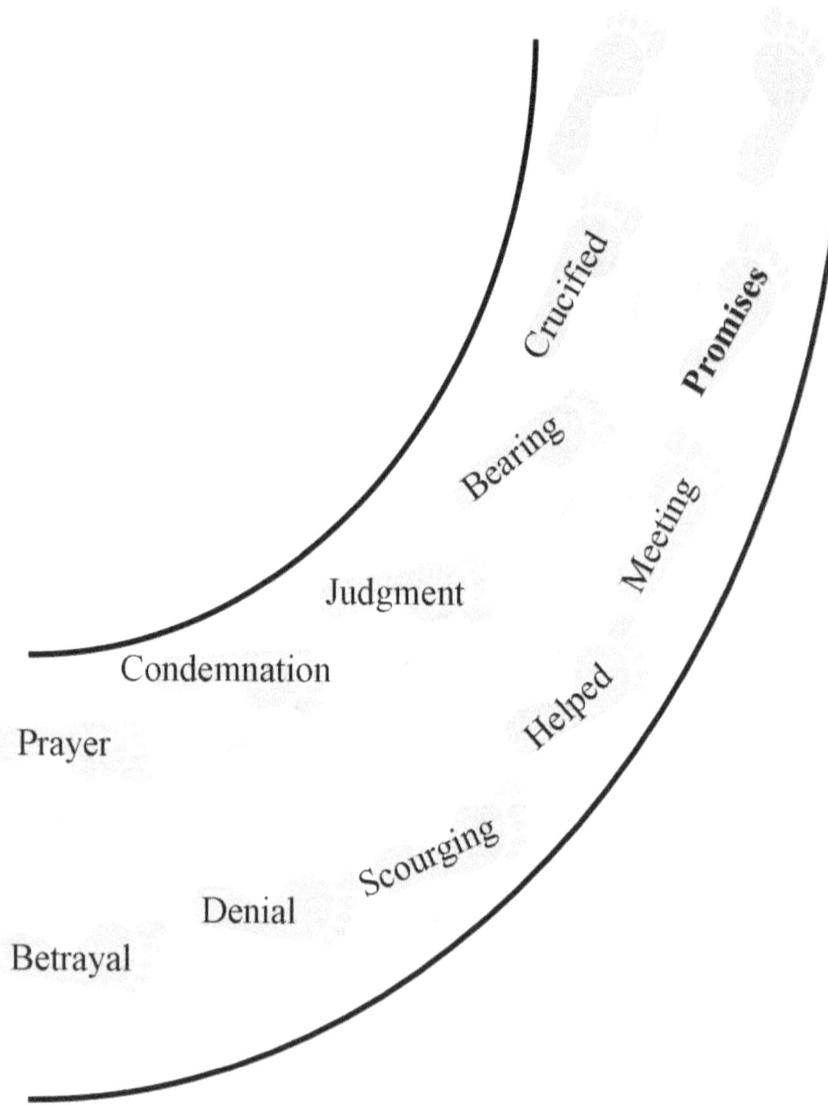

You are going to discover that when you are in your condemnation, there will always be someone who has either experienced the same kind of scrutiny or is currently going through it. Even though they may be guilty of what they were accused of they still will understand your pain and try to comfort you during your situation. Sometimes, people can become bitter and angry of what they are experiencing and hold grudges against the whole world and are unable to hold sensible conversations with anyone.

Jesus is hanging between two, guilty prisoners. One on the left and one on the right. The one on the left had the audacity to poke fun and antagonize Jesus for what He is facing. What nerve of him to ridicule Jesus when he is in the same condemnation. Some people who have suffered what you are experiencing will celebrate your demise, because misery loves company. The enemy attempted to break the spirit of Jesus by identifying Him with criminals and bringing upon Him the same kind of torture as they. The thief on the left had a broken spirit and therefore, found justification in criticizing someone else. Don't give these kinds of people the time or day.

Jesus ignores this man because he doesn't have any room to condemn anybody. Don't pay any attention to the bad thief, but have conversation with the good thief (*repented person*).

The good thief will affirm and defend you, while the bad thief will mock and criticize you. When the thief on the right, heard what the other thief said: he immediately told him that what he was doing was wrong and that he had no room to even begin to say anything concerning the accusation's of Jesus.

This good thief had remorse for what he had done and showed forth a repented heart for the crimes he had committed. He took responsibility for what he had done and even said, he deserved what was coming to him, but rebuked the approach that the bad thief had taken, against Jesus.

Doesn't it feel good to finally find someone who recognizes what they have done and where they are, but if given a second chance, would make a complete turnaround? God will typically have someone with you who understand your dilemma and will provide you some level of comfort, by speaking to your heart. This moved Jesus and provided some sense of empowerment to Him.

The good thief says: **Lord, when you come into your destiny, please don't forget about me.** Finally! Somebody who believes in you and knows that it's not over for you. Imagine what this does for Jesus. Someone who recognizes that they are standing next to divinity and in the company of an unbreakable, anointing!

As you are hanging there, wondering if anyone gets it, God soon reminds you that there is a legitimate reason as to why you are going through what you are going through. Even if it's just one, it's worth it! If there is ever a question in Jesus mind, if His sacrifice mattered, God reveals through the guilty, sinner that it's worth it. The thief looks beyond the natural and perceives the spiritual. And subjects himself to the ruler ship of Jesus and makes a faithful request, to bid him permission to join Him in His destined, place.

I love the fact that God has someone there to not only believe in you, but also within your destiny. Those who are willing to share in your suffering will also be the ones who share in your glory. If they cannot support you in your pain, they don't deserve to bask in your reign!

Jesus does not lose his passion, desire, commitment and vision of His destiny in the midst of torture and pain. Jesus is hopeful and makes a promise to a thief, while in the worst, possible position to be in. The enemy wants to torture you so bad, to the point that you forget all about your opportunities, hopes and dreams and not even mention your destiny. With great faith and confidence, you must be willing to speak those things that be not, as though they were.

In other words, despite what it looks like can you still speak God's blessings over your life? You cannot lose sight of your destiny and give up in your struggle and lose voice to God's Promise. Promise the people, who are fully in it with you that they will share in your destined place. People don't forget powerful words that have been spoken to them. God's Word sticks with you through thick and thin. It is what inspires you, while you are facing tough times and it provokes assurance to those who trust in you and what has come out of your mouth.

Jesus says: **this day, you will be with me in paradise!**

In the midst of what you are going through, your destined place is just waiting on you to believe in it and speak into the atmosphere. Your place of destiny is framed by the words that come out of your own mouth. Thank God for people who believe in you and the blessings that God has for you, but will you be able to believe and speak of your destiny for yourself? With great confidence, Jesus says to him: that as soon as this is over, I'll see you in my destined place and there is a place just for you. Never lose your ability to prophetically, speak of your outcome in the midst of pain and suffering. You are not speaking your own outcomes into existence, but what God has said or shown concerning you of your destiny.

I remember in 2011 when I was diagnosed with High Blood Pressure and my doctor put me on a certain pill that produced a cough as a side effect. I coughed so much that I lost my voice for an entire month and I couldn't preach God's Word. Praise God, I had other associates who could fill in for me and proclaim His Words to our congregation. But being a preacher and unable to speak God's Word was devastating for me. The enemy tried to kill my voice and rob the church of what God had put in my mouth.

What are you doing during your time of suffering, that as a result of side effects, it's causing you to lose your prophetic voice? What God has put in your mouth is a blessing, not only for you, but for those who are suffering too. Keep speaking your destiny! Speak of the celebration that's going to take place as soon as you get out of this!

When Jesus spoke of His destined place, he said it loud enough to where the good thief could hear Him, but low enough to where the naysayers could not.

Are you speaking loud enough to where your followers can hear you?

Question 1: What did Jesus have to go through?
**The willingness of believing and speaking His destiny, regardless of
His situation.** You must not lose hope in the midst of tragedy and
circumstance. Expectation builds your faith in that which you
cannot see and allows you to have confidence in what God has said.

Question 2: Who or What was His opposition?
While going through, you will typically have a good and bad voice in
your ear. **He was mocked by the bad thief and ridiculed for his
current situation.** Despite what others are saying, you must listen
to the expectations of others and gain strength in what God has said
concerning you.

 Question 3: What was the practical example He set?
**He let the bad thief have his fun, ignored him and spoke where he
had an audience.** Do not give time or day to those who poke fun or
disbelieve in your destiny. Keep looking to God by hearing the
expectations of others and their support and confidence in you.

Question 4: What was the Spiritual significance?
**The enemy will try to silence your faith and close up your ears, in
an attempt to cause you to abandon your expectations in God.**
Paradise was meant for Jesus and His followers! If you speak and
declare God's Word of Truth, you will always have someone to
celebrate with!

STEP 12

Jesus Speaks To His Mother and The Beloved Disciple
John 19:25-27

(Your Commitment To Connect People
Together, Before You Depart)

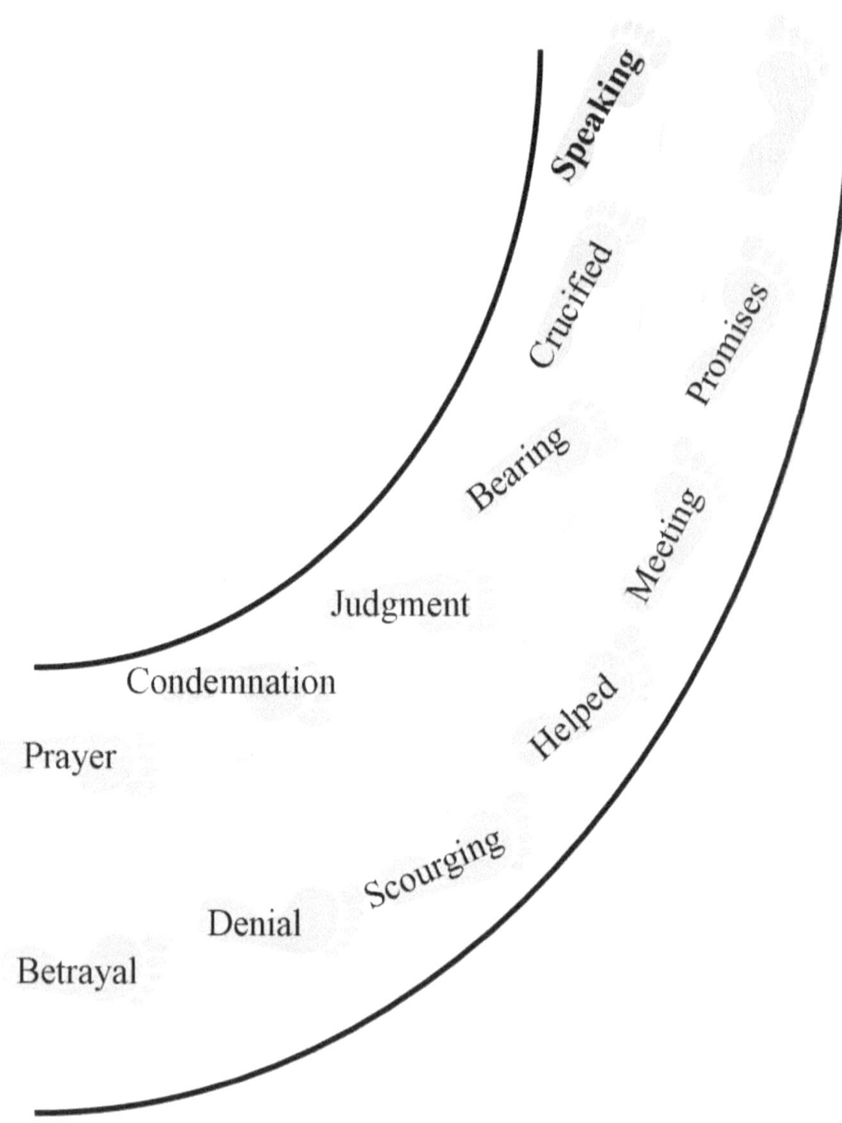

I don't care what the situation is it's extremely hard to say "Goodbye." There is no worse feeling than having to say goodbye to someone you love, appreciate and cherish. It hurts like heck. All of what you've accomplished and been through together and now it has to come to an end. To have to watch someone deteriorate right before your eyes and know that at some point, you're going to have to say goodbye, is a very difficult thing to do.

Despite all of your enemies, experiences, setbacks, naysayers and haters, there are still people who truly do love you and hate to see you go. It's your choice. You don't have to leave, if you don't want to. All you have to do is just change your mind or keep fighting for survival. The reality is: you have to go and more than anyone, you know you have to go, so if that be the case, it is your responsibility to connect people together in relationships that will fill the empty voids in their lives.

This is a tough, but necessary stage within life or ministry to go through. Jesus is looking at His mother and His mother is looking at Him. He is suffering and her heart is melting. His closest follower is looking at Him and He is looking at His follower and His follower is in disbelief.

Why does it have to come to this? Why should it have to come to an end, so soon? We need more time. There was so much I wanted to say to them and they wanted to say to me and instead of the usual get together, we always anticipated, we are faced with having to plan a funeral or a going away party.

It is next to impossible to hold back the tears.

Can you remember all of the times you had to say goodbye? Whether it was moving to a new neighborhood, changing an occupation, separating from a significant other, stepping down from a ministry or even changing churches. This is hard stuff.

You know you have control over those kinds of situations, when your heart is at peace and because you realize that life must go on without you, you take the necessary time to connect the ones you love and appreciate and build relationships for future success. Jesus shows us how to connect people, together before He left.

He gives permission to His mother to embrace someone else she can love like a son and He gives permission to His spiritual brother to embrace His mother, like his mother and take care of her in His absence. Joseph, who was Jesus' stepfather, was no longer around. Historical documents assumed he had died and left her as a single mother. Besides that, Joseph was with her from the very beginning with Jesus and knew the anointing that was upon His life, even as a baby.

Mother Mary never forgot the divine revelation's she received regarding Jesus and she always kept them within her heart. What is she going to do? Where is she going to go? What hope will she have after Jesus is gone? Jesus understands her dilemma and makes sure that He replaces His vacancy with someone He loves and can trust to take care of the one He loved.

At this stage, it is necessary to know what people need and be willing to connect the right people together. If your heart is in what you are doing and you truly care about future ministry, you must prepare someone to take your place. You never know when or if you have to return from the place you left, so it is very important that when you leave, you show your concern for others and try as best you can to replace your spirit with a likeminded spirit.

All of what you accomplished and prepared will be for nothing if you don't prepare a replacement. If what you've started dies after your gone, than you have failed. This was a brief ceremony of affirmation for the people He loved. He made sure they both knew they needed each other and what they had in common was what they both experienced, together.

All of what we have been taught by God is really all about building, strong relationships. The strongest expression of love is your ability to connect people together. If your ministry or service is going to continue, even after your gone, you must rally people together and inspire them to value each other in a very real and personal way.

Don't be so overcome and consumed with your own struggles that you forget to invest in the people who have supported you when things were going well and not so well. Be sure to separate your enemies from your friends and don't treat everyone as your enemy, just because you may be hurting. Don't make your ministry suffer because you are leaving. Yes. I know who you are makes it unique, but your name is on the line and the historical witness of your service.

Even though you are leaving, leave your spirit behind and let the moral and ethical values, remain and provide a pathway for fulfillment.

Remember, the people you leave behind are in a war zone. A position where others may not value them because they value you and after you are gone, who is going to validate, inspire and encourage them?

Right now, they need you more than you need them. You are going to go on within the next phase of life, while they are left behind to deal with a hostile crowd. Encourage them to stick together and not forget who they are and what they are called to do. The enemy is after what you have started and it is his attempt for what you have done, to end with you. The enemy wants you to take with you, what you started, so that he can promote his own destructive, manipulative agenda and take back complete control of the people who have made progress, as a result of your leadership or friendship.

Your commitment is not so much to the ones who hurt you, but the ones who helped you. Don't let them down by not reassembling them together and reinforcing the need to keep the good things going. Where there is unity, there is strength! They cannot do it if they are divided, but they can do it if they are united.

When you left, for whatever reason, did the good thing remain and continue on in progression?

If not, who didn't you connect before you left?

1.

2.

3.

Question 1: What did Jesus have to go through?
Observing people, He really loved, watch Him deteriorate and
pass away. When everybody is hurting, there should always be a
moment of silence, but the ones who do not perceive themselves
as victims, encourage others to keep living, beyond their absence.
Life must go on!

 Question 2: Who or What was His opposition?
Jesus was faced with an uncaring spirit. Either He could say: I
don't care and die or leave. Or He could say: I do care and die or
leave with dignity, by preparing the ones He loved for His
departure. Connect your support system together and encourage
them to stick together and carry on the spirit of what you started.

Question 3: What was the practical example He set?
He put aside His own feelings and charged His mother and
personal friend to embrace each other with a future commitment
of unity. Jesus chooses John, The Beloved to take His place in being
a son to His mother. He was socially, spiritually and emotionally,
putting His mother within a line of inheritance. How many people
die or move on without leaving the people they love behind with
nothing?

Question 4: What was the Spiritual significance?
Mary gave birth to The Savior, The Anointed One and the enemy
wanted to abort her faith in what she gave birth to. When you
have given birth to anointed, purpose the enemy will try his best to
destroy the power of your testimony. *Transfer your anointing*
within the hearts of others!

STEP 13

Jesus Dies on The Cross

Matthew 27:45 - 54

(Your Commitment To Yield Yourself Into The Hands of God)

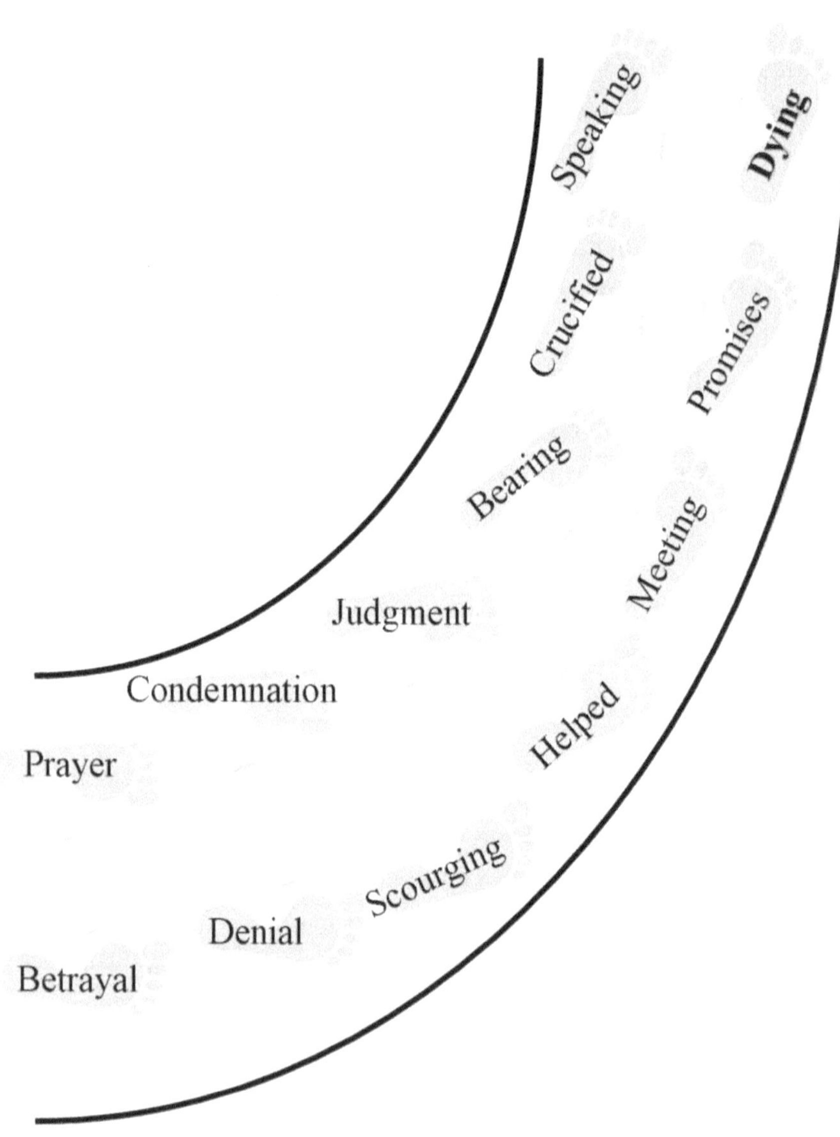

Hope is always in the air until it actually happens, when finality occurs and death removes you out of the way. Death is inevitable and at some point the death angel will arrive, whether it's separating the spirit from the flesh or something coming to an end. Death is actually, a part of life. Every birthday will have its death day and unfortunately, all things must come to an end.

In this story, we find that at a very unusual time of the day (high noon) the whole land was in complete darkness. What a strange phenomenon. And Jesus cries out: My God, My God. Why have you deserted me? Not that death was strange, but at the time in which it occurred, is what made it strange. Death seems to show up at the wrong time, one day or moment when all seems well. When you think everything is going great! Your job seems to be happy. The church seems to be growing and ministry seems to be enriching and then all of a sudden, death (finality) occurs.

It is at that moment when a person feels as though, God has deserted them and left them all alone, to die for unjust or unwarranted reasons. When Jesus died, he felt the separation of His Spirit from His flesh and the force of internal, conflict was overwhelming. From this account, we come to understand that when a person dies, his spirit is in a conflict.

Haven't you felt it? When finality occurs and that groaning and moaning of conflict takes place within you, it sometimes causes you to scream out or yell in great agony or frustration. It's a spiritual thing. I have found myself there, when I have had all I can handle and what I've worked so hard to accomplish doesn't seem like it's going to make it and all I can do is yell or scream with moaning's and groaning's that cannot be uttered. It happens when relationships come to an end, when people we know and love, pass away, when we get released from a job, rejected for a loan and etc. It happens and if we are not careful, the agony can push us to do things that harm ourselves or those around us. It's a spiritual thing.

Jesus felt it and if it was strong enough to cause Him to yell, surely it will force us to do the same thing. But what I love about Jesus' is that He always went a step further. Jesus did one more thing that saved Him, just before He dies. This is the one thing that is so critical for us to do, if we want to stay alive, even after death or finality happens in our life. Jesus says: *Father, into your hands I commit my Spirit!*

Before finality occurs to the death of a ministry or relationship, don't die, before giving your spirit to God. When you give your spirit to God, even in the midst of death, God will sustain you and keep you alive (encouraged) while death has taken place. When this takes place, the shell, covering or outward body lies dormant, but the Spirit is yet alive.

If you fail to commit your spirit to The Lord, as the natural dies, your spirit is subject to dying with it. That's what leads to depression and suicide. When a person's spirit dies, it is extremely hard to value anything worth living. The enemy not only wants to break your spirit, but also, destroy your spirit.

While in the hands of God, He will minister to your Spirit and give you real meaning for existence. You soon understand that when something dies, yet you give yourself to God, t your Spirit is in another dimension and there is yet and still work to be done.

The work that you are doing now is not out front, visible work, but work behind the scene or beneath the surface of what has died. When Jesus died the bible says that He went into hades and set the captives free. The captives were those who died, prior to His death, burial and ultimate, resurrection. There are folks who have spiritually, died as a result of finality and it is your job to raise them up to a level of inspiration and motivation.

Even though people could no longer see Jesus, physically ministering, it did not prohibit Him from working beyond death. You can too! During this stage of finality and death, you must give your Spirit into the hands of God and continue your assignment, below the surface of public manifestation. You are the catalyst in providing an open door for all of those who have given up, lost hope and died, when their project died.

Remember, this is the time where your support system is mourning your loss and the naysayers and enemies are celebrating your demise, so this is the time where there is public silence. This is not the time to try to defend yourself or talk about what you could, should or wouldn't do, but this is a time of silence. Stay quiet and work behind the scene. Let God restore and revive your situation, so when the time is right, you can come forth.

The text also says; that graves were opened, and the bodies of many holy people who had died were raised to life. Oh yes! This is the time when you are investing in someone else's ministry or someone else's life, in the process of their resurrection. Shh! Don't say anything, just help someone else to revive and when your enemies and naysayers least expect it, here you come!

Some believer's really struggle with this principle because they are use to being out front or in charge. Instead of taking a low place, they opt completely, out and forfeit the opportunity to invest in someone else.   If truth be told, some things need to die. Some things need to come to an end and that's ok. When something has fulfilled its life cycle, it's typical that it must come to an end, but can reinvent itself through some other form. We will talk about this later, but just know that you have the power to still stay in control, but just realizing that your role has changed.

And that role has now become in the form of a supporting cast to previous believer's who's spirits has died as a result of something dying or coming to an end in their life. Look at how many ministries can evolve, spirits receive renewal and hearts become encouraged? You are still a great asset, even though what you have led has died. Before your death or finality takes place, please don't forget to release your Spirit into the hands of God and let God sustain you while you are healing and working underground.

Do I have the courage to recognize when finality is taking place and submit my Spirit to God?

What has been the result when I did not give (*yield*) my Spirit to God, before finality took place?

Question 1: What did Jesus have to go through?
Not prolonging death, when He knew death was inevitable. As difficult as it may be to call it quits, one should not try to hold on to something too long when they know it's over. Sometimes one can stay too long or try too hard in order to not become an embarrassment in the eyes of others. Know when your time is up and don't be afraid or ashamed to let something die that needs to die.

 Question 2: Who or What was His opposition?
The spirit of pride was His opposition. Either He could refuse to die or humble Himself and finish the sacrifice.
You are your biggest enemy. This is all about how you manage yourself during the time of great loss. Humility is the great defender of pride. When you operate within a spirit of humility, you possess the power to do whatever is necessary for the right circumstances. *Humility does not mean weakness, but power under control!*

Question 3: What was the practical example He set?
Jesus had to make a conscious decision to live, despite dying, by putting His Spirit into the control of God.
I know it hurts. I know its tuff, but Father I give myself to you and ask that you give me the strength and courage to live on, in Jesus name, Amen!

Question 4: What was the Spiritual significance?
The enemy's ploy is to destroy your witness of giving back and to keep hostage the many ministries that have died before you. Go down and minister to them and bring them back up with you, as much as possible.

STEP 14

Jesus Is Placed In The Tomb

Luke 23:50 - 54

(The Temporary Place, That's Not Yours)

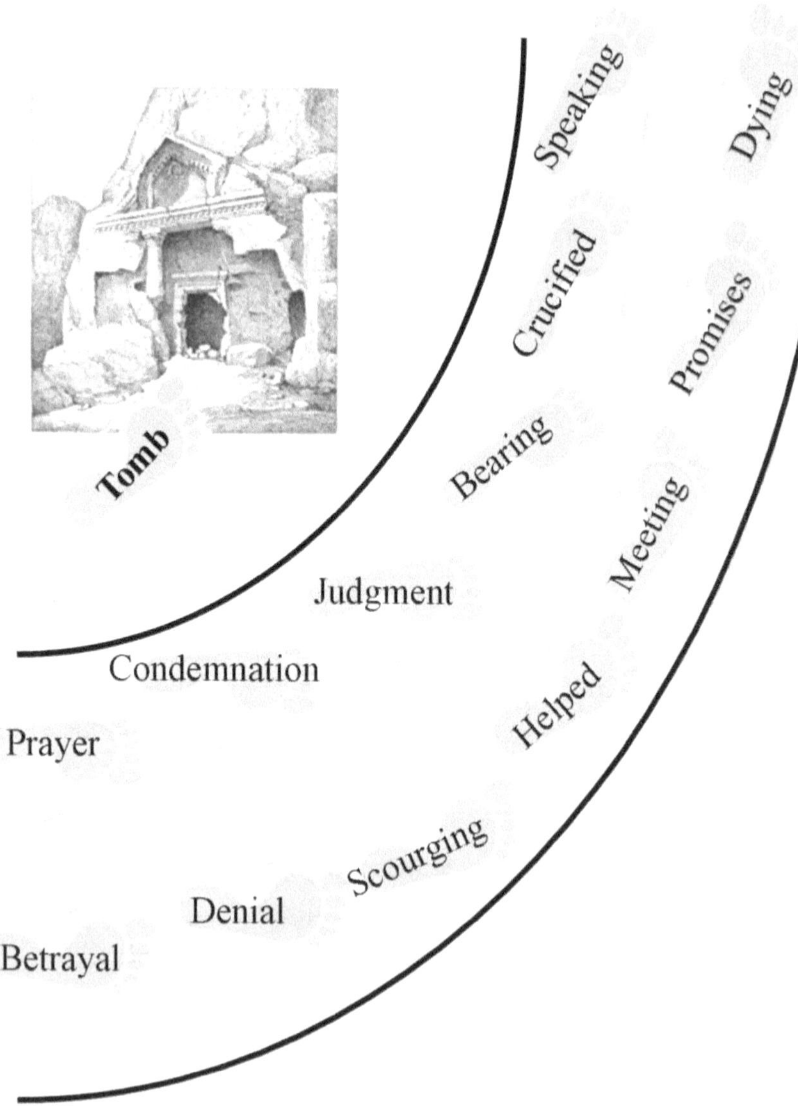

While the Spirit of Jesus is now loosing the spirits of those captive, free, His physical body lies, limp and lifeless on the tree. His body is taken down and expected to be taken to the graveyard and placed within a tomb. However, a leader of the Sanhedrin Council comes and requests His body in order to give Him a decent, respectful burial and makes the decision to place Him in the tomb that he had purchased for himself.

This tomb was prophetically on loan to Jesus and only served as a temporary holding place for a temporary death state. Did you hear that? Your temporary silent place is only a temporary death state! You are destined to rise again! Your Spirit may no longer be within the framework of what was physically manifested and because your spirit didn't die when the thing you were connected to died, that thing seems to now lay dormant and limp from your absence or lack of influence and now the silence of your absence is within the process of being forgotten, by covering it up and closing it in to only memories of the dark past.

You can't fight against it, because you are no longer in it and since its come to finality, all we can do is wrap it up, close it up and seal it up. But this tomb is not for you! This isn't your tomb and since it's not your tomb, there are other plans for this tomb and you being in it forever, is not it. The fact of the matter is: this tomb is designed for someone else's burial and you must not outlive your stay. Someone else is coming here and the plot has their name on it and not yours.

Stop claiming someone else's space of no return and claim your day of victory! This is a temporary visit and when your spirit is revitalized within your body, new life can began!

Jesus is placed within the tomb and He is left within the tomb, within a cave, where darkness and silence reside. But this tomb belonged to Joseph, who was yet living and out of his love and respect for Jesus, he let Him borrow his tomb until he was ready for it, himself. Isn't it amazing that the people who carry us into our tombs are the ones who we think should go before us? They are naturally called, pall bearers. They gather around on each side and are called to carry us into our gravesite since we cannot carry ourselves.

Thank God for your pall bearers! The people who are assigned, to carry you when you cannot carry yourself. The ones who love you and support you and wish at any moment, you could just rise up and go on as if you've never had to suffer death or demise at all. They are carrying you with this great deal of hurt and pain, while also carrying a wish or desire for your resurrection.

Because one is not consciously, aware of who is carrying them they have no idea of the motive or intents of the ones who's holding them up. It's typically not your enemies who will carry you because their job is over. They have welcomed and waited for your demise or destroyed you from the existence of your ministry and influence, so they won't bother to carry the empty, limp and lifeless shell of what remains from your leadership.

In this case, Joseph believed in Jesus and I believe, he believed in His resurrection, so if resurrection was going to happen, let it happen in a place that belongs to me! Because if He gets up in my dead place, I know that there is hope for me! This was an honor for Joseph and an opportunity to be recorded in his historical legacy as the man who gave up his tomb for the one who had power over the tomb and walked away from the grips of death and right into the realm of eternal life. This is the anticipated hope that Joseph has and the bible says that he begged for the body of Jesus. This, my friends is the validation that God will give you when you have died from something that was strong enough to kill your spirit. People will beg for you even though you are no longer in operation, position or ministry.

Do you have value, beyond the grave? Is it an honor for people to carry your legacy and not let what you've accomplished go unnoticed or forgotten? Joseph said: Jesus is dead, but this is my tomb. In other words, He's dead right now, but that's not going to always be the case. He's going to give it back to me, after He uses it for His glory and purpose, then He will return it back to its rightful owner.

Thank God for people who prepare for their departure and are not so selfish as to not allow others to use what they are not currently, using for themselves. One day Joseph will need his tomb, but in the meantime he gives permission for the body of Jesus to lay there. How many folk will just let you rest in a quiet place until you are able to get back up, again? How many people will not charge you for using their space as a temporary place for you?

A true friend says: I'm with you and I support you and whatever you need, I got it and until you are able to get back up on your feet, you don't owe me a thing! What's mine is yours and I am willing to help you in any way I can. That's incredible! And believe me when I tell you; there is a special place for people such as this.

Your temporary tomb or holding place is not yours, forever. It's just a place where God wants to glorify Himself, by raising you up. Don't take ownership of what's not yours and take ownership of who God is in your life! Thank God that you have somewhere to rest until you're able to get back up again.

Joseph's tomb is designed for him, not you. Don't try to place permanent, affixtures within somebody else's home. Stop putting doubt and hopelessness in somebody else's tomb. Reclaim your joy, reestablish your faith, encourage your hope and disconnect your fears and shame of defeat. Get yourself ready to get up again and walk into your destiny!

 You were only there for a season and this place is necessary for your journey as God gets ready to raise you up from the thing that killed your dreams, your goals, your ministry, your family, your relationship, your career. Don't own complete, failure! Don't own defeat, forever. You will rise again!

Who has been a temporary resting place for you when demise, seemed final?

1.

2.

3.

Were or are they a part of the Sanhedrin Council (*governing leadership of church life*)?

Question 1: What did Jesus have to go through?
Allowing someone else to carry Him while He lay dormant.
Sometimes pride gets in the way of our permitting someone to carry
us at our very weakest moments. We fight against the privilege of
others who see it as an honor to carry us when we cannot do for
ourselves. Just be still.

Question 2: Who or What was His opposition?
Permanency of a death or holding place was His opposition. It is
defeats' job to try and block you for good and keep you lifeless,
without any hope of resurrecting, but you must not become
satisfied with staying down.

Question 3: What was the practical example He set?
**Remain patient, still and quiet during your burial and don't try to
resurrect too soon.** Believe in yourself and wait on the timing of
God. If you try to get up too soon, you risk rising, before your new
purpose is ready for you. Be still and know that He is God and let
the manifestation of your new purpose, shape itself within your role
in destiny.

Question 4: What was the Spiritual significance?
**The temporary holding place is not familiar with who you are and
cannot keep you because it does not know you.** Don't give
permanent, defeat too much credit and allow it to keep you down.
You are the light! Navigate your way out of that dark place and
present yourself back to the world in which you left, but with
renewed, authority!

DESTINY!

John 20:1-18

(When Your Resurrection Comes As A Result of Your Necessary Journey)

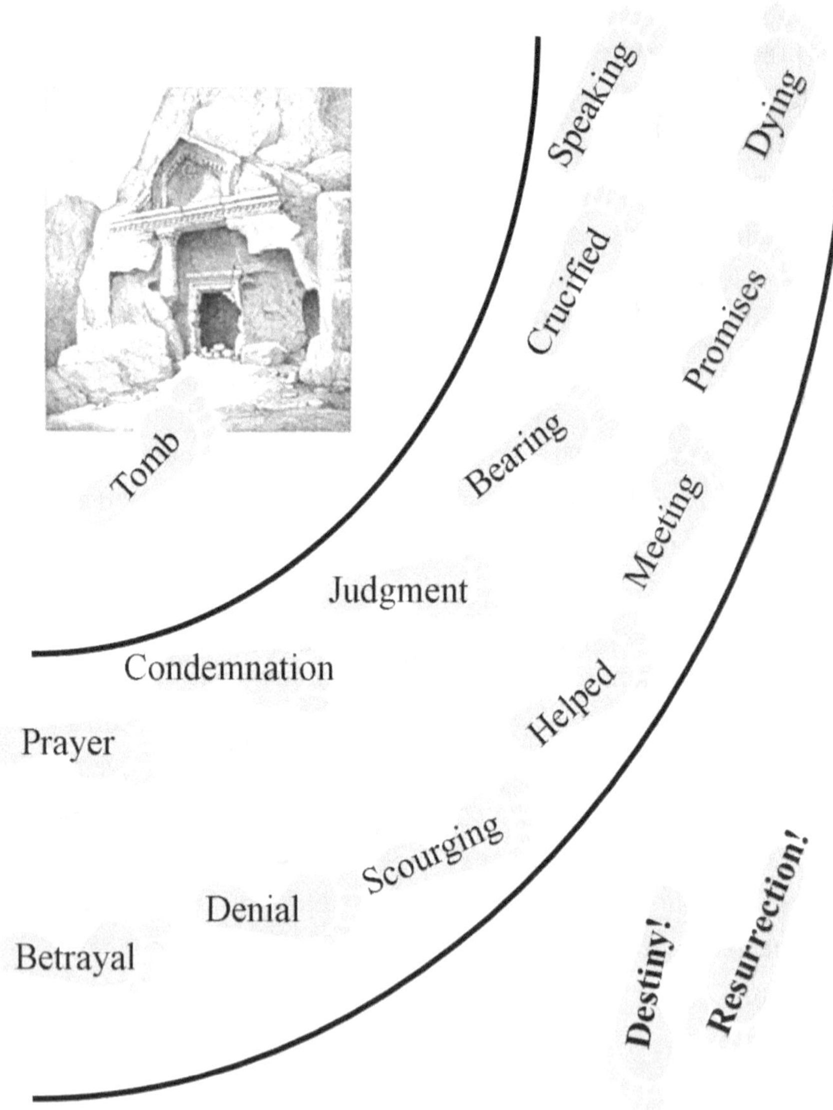

Resurrection happens within the quietness and stillness of time, but the manifestation is open for the world to see! Historically, speaking it seems that Jesus rose up out of the grave between 5:30-6:00 am. Very early in the morning when the birds began to sing their morning medley. The scripture says that the stone had been rolled away! The stone was not rolled away so that Jesus could get out, but that the world could come in and witness the blessing of Jesus being removed from the state and place of death.

Notice that its not the enemy who initially, detects the absence of who was dead, but the loving, support system of those who were coming to complete the burial process by anointing his body with sweet spice aroma's. Their reverence and respect for what was dead is what caused them to make death not look and smell so bad. The enemy doesn't care and it is his job to make it look and feel worse than what it already is. Thank God for people who will try to make the best out of a bad situation and try their best to finalize a situation, so that the taste or smell is not so unbearable.

Jesus had already foretold, He would die and yet rise again, but people didn't believe Him or take Him seriously. When you understand that going into your destiny, requires much sacrifice, then you also know it may require the death of something or the persecution of something. But you must also prophetically, speak of your resurrection! Folks may not believe you, but you must believe in your God and know that what He allowed you to go through was not designed to keep you!

When the ones who loved Jesus had approached the tomb and saw that the stone was rolled away and that His body was no longer in the grips of silence, and idleness, two angels were left in the tomb to testify to the resurrection of Jesus. What I am saying is that God will always leave a witness to the fact that what use to have you, no longer does and where you use to be is not where you are now. Praise God for always leaving a witness to validate that death and defeat is no longer the end of our story, but life, authority and destiny is what we are operating in now!

The angels invited them to come and see where death, lay, and when they investigated they saw the swads of death clothes that was wrapped around His body and the napkin that was laid over His eyes, but they had no evidence of a body. The swads of clothes that they saw was within the shape of a cocoon. It looked like a body and was shaped like a body, but what looked final, sealed and full was empty. What remained was just the shell of what used to have Him bound.

When resurrection takes place, the shell or cocoon of what use to have you will draw people to it, only to find that you are no longer in it. You have gotten up from your still and dead place and are now empowered to function in the destiny of who and what God made you to be!

The authority of Jesus was now completely, beyond human or natural ability. He didn't need the stone to be rolled away, so that He could get up and go out, but now He has the authority to walk through stone brick, walls and death. Because the authority He is operating in is not natural or human, but spiritual. Can I encourage you again? That even though your body may lay in physical or natural situations, your Spirit can be free! Just because your body is bound does not mean that your Spirit has to be bound.

Just because your situation has power, does not mean that you don't have the power to not be utterly, affected by it. The greatest enemy that the world has ever known, has now been proven weak and unable to hold Jesus back. Death is defeated! Oh death, where is your sting. Oh grave, where is your victory?

When you are resurrected, it's time for you to celebrate your comeback. Gather those around you who have supported you and encouraged you and did not give up on you and even though you suffered loss, they still respected you, carried you, remembered you and cared for you, especially when it was the end for you. You are now the living evidence that God can and will raise His children from the state and place of defeat and death!

This is not the time for you to be quiet. This is not the time for you to stay to yourself and mourn your experience. Come out and tell the world what God has done. Make your way to the church and testify to the Goodness of God and how He brought you through the storms and rains of opposition and demise and lifted you up, out of the grips of death and defeat and have now granted you the authority to operate and experience your destiny!

Take off what had you down and put on what you're wearing in your new place. Affirm those who still can't believe what God has done for you. Let them know that God is true and that He is a rewarder of them that diligently, seek Him.

I have one more very important principle to share with you and I pray you listen very closely.

In John 20:19-23 Jesus does something that we all can take notice of and replicate, after we have been resurrected from our state and places of defeat and death.

He shows up in the midst of His support system and the very first thing He does, without question or hesitation, He shows them His SCARS. The scars are reminders of the pain and suffering, experiences that you have gone through. They are the identifiers of the struggles of what we all have to go through in life and the church. They are really, conversation starters that are designed to lead us into sharing our hope and faith with those who may still be suffering.

The scars only tell where He has been, but had no power over where He was going. The scars do not define who He is, but only tell where He's been and what He's been through. And if God is going to raise you up, you must not be ashamed to share your scars. They are testimonies of what God has brought you through and you must not be afraid to let people see them and touch them.

It's now a scar. That means at one point, it was a wound. A wound is still open and possibly still bleeding, but a scar has been healed and only exist for you to tell the story of what you had to go through in order to get to where you are now. Those scars made you! Those scars matured you! Those scars don't hurt anymore! Those scars have now blended into the fabric of your total being and now when someone asks you about it, you can talk about it and tell them what your God has done for you!

Conclusion and Final Thoughts!

by

Dr. Kevin L. Harris Sr., Senior Pastor

I hope and pray that this writing has been beneficial for every person that has read it. I know that many people have experienced some very difficult challenges within the church and I know that your perception of the church has been shaped by the many bad experiences you may have had.

I am here to tell you that there is no place like the church! Yes. The church has done some bad things, but give them credit for the many good things, too. The church is a place where people of all kinds of walks of life, race, culture and beliefs, attend. It is the melting pot of human culture and a place that takes people in as they are, in an attempt to develop them into who God wants them to be.

Along the way, mistakes will happen. Hurt will occur and opposition and persecution will take place, but don't run from it and miss out on your development. How is it that people can carry so much thick skin when they function on their jobs, families or social environments, but when they come to the church they become so sensitive and walk away at the growl of a gnat? No local church is perfect. No child of God is completely, without sin. Some are more mature than others. Some have a more pleasant disposition than others, but if you walk away from the church and claim that nobody is right, what kind of attitude has come upon you that makes you right and everybody else wrong?

It may be revealed, that you are just like them and God maybe showing you, "you". Don't allow what people do or don't do; determine what you are going to do for God. Remember, in the end, its God who you are hurting and giving up on, not man. Why does God get the blame for what people do?

I am telling you that God allows us to go through these things because they are necessary for our spiritual growth and interaction between humanity. He went through it and requires us to do it as well.

Think about it. He subjected Himself to the people He created and allowed them to misuse and abuse Him. Yet He forgave them for everything they did to Him and still sacrificed Himself, on the cross in the event they wanted to accept, embrace and appreciate His love for them.

All along your necessary journey, God truly, understands and He wants you to know that He is right there with you every step of the way. Each stage of your experience, He is teaching you what to do, how to do it and what to look for and who to look for.

The church can become better, because you have been made better! If you hang in there and overcome your obstacles, you take the ministry or church to another level of maturity and you then become a teacher of spiritual development for the body of Christ. Those who have walked away from the church because of hurt and pain may still be wandering in a place of unforgiveness or isolation.

You can inspire them back into the activity of church life, through the sharing of your experiences and resurrection of your own knowledge and understanding, regarding church and the challenges within the ministry. Go get them and tell them to follow your lead, as you lead them back to church life and help them to grow beyond hurt and pain.

These challenges may or may not happen in this order, but it is certain you will experience each stage in ministry. People have walked away from the church because of these experiences, expecting something other than this, but let me tell you, these stages are completely, necessary for your development in your faith and life.

Your ability to overcome each of these stages and fulfill some of the challenging stages is the very first step and that's PRAYER. Since prayer is the very first step and doesn't cause you to become so vulnerable within the elevation of problems, it requires you to bend down and kneel upon your knees. Pray that God blocks the challenges from you and prepare you for your journey.

God is preparing you for your destiny, but it requires the experience of these stages. Many people have quit in ministry or walked away from the church because of these experiences. I don't care what church you go to or what state or country it is in, you will have to go through these stages of ministry in order to get to your destined place.

So pick yourself back up! Go back to church! Get back in that ministry and understand the battle in which you are in. The church is your training ground, the place that will develop your character and spiritual fortitude.

Companies will only train you for their specific needs, but the church will train you to deal with any and every challenge you face in life. Apologize to God, yourself, your Pastor and Ministry and get back in pursuit of your destiny!

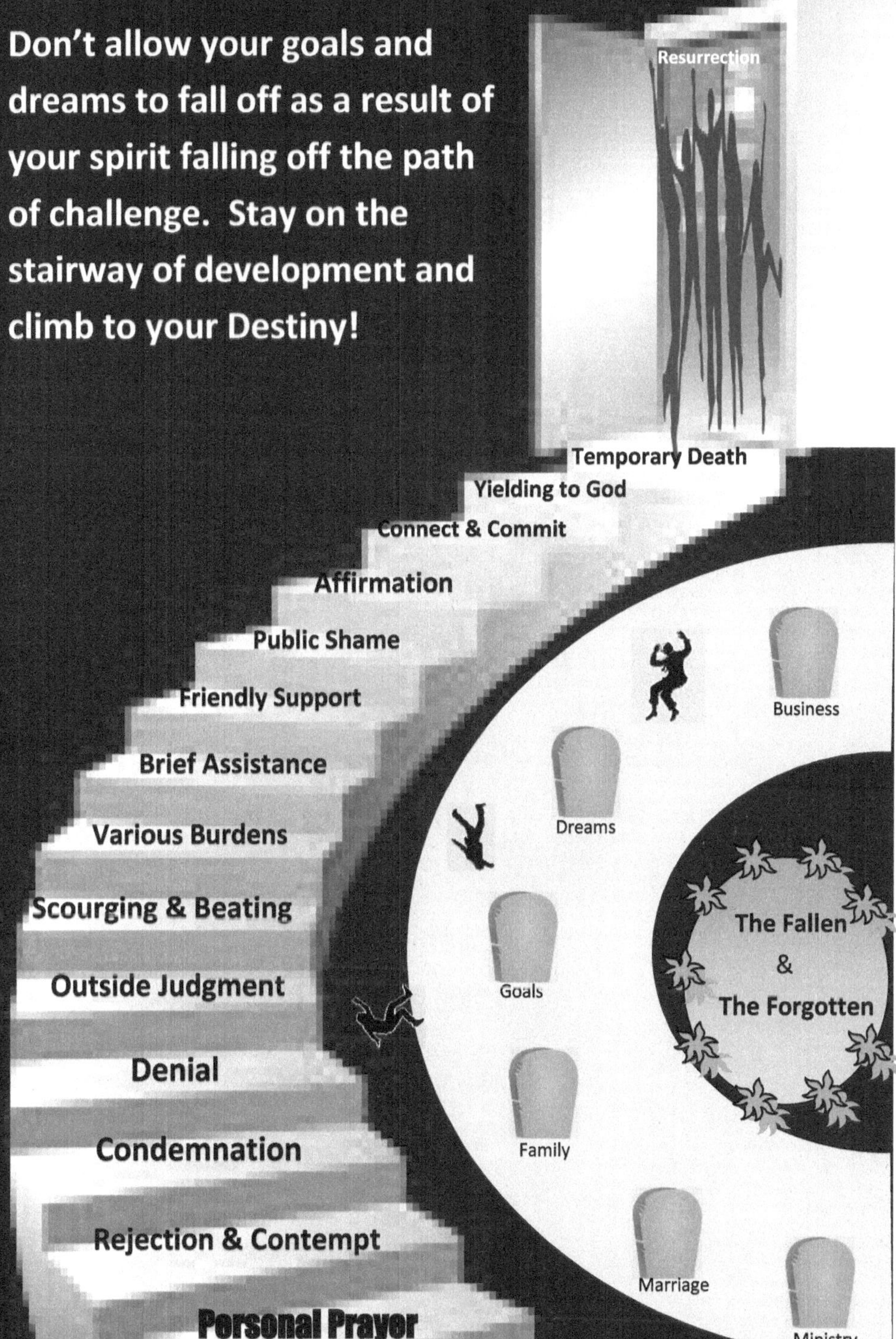

Don't allow your goals and dreams to fall off as a result of your spirit falling off the path of challenge. Stay on the stairway of development and climb to your Destiny!
Resurrection
Temporary Death
Yielding to God
Connect & Commit
Affirmation
Public Shame
Friendly Support
Brief Assistance
Various Burdens
Scourging & Beating
Outside Judgment
Denial
Condemnation
Rejection & Contempt
Personal Prayer
Business
Dreams
Goals
Family
Marriage
Ministry
The Fallen
&
The Forgotten

THE END!

Your situation was designed

to **"MAKE You"**

not break you!

By

Dr. Kevin L. Harris Sr.

9 780986 408700